Gambling on her Panther

Book 3
Shifters in Vegas

by Anna Lowe

Editing by Lisa A. Hollett

Cover design by Jacqueline Sweet

Contents

Other books in this series

Shifters in Vegas

Paranormal romance with a zany twist

Gambling on Trouble

Gambling on Her Dragon

Gambling on Her Bear

Gambling on Her Panther

www.annalowebooks.com

Free Books

Get your free e-books now!

Sign up for my newsletter at *annalowebooks.com* to get three free books!

- *Desert Wolf*: Friend or Foe (Book 1.1 in the Twin Moon Ranch series)

- *Off the Charts* (the prequel to the Serendipity Adventure series)

- *Perfection* (the prequel to the Blue Moon Saloon series)

Chapter One

"Hit me," the young honeymooner in a cheap suit announced.

Behind him, lights flashed as a middle-aged woman at a slot machine came up with three in a row, winning... Well, not enough to retire on, but enough for a good story to take home from her trip to Las Vegas.

Dex pinned the honeymooner with a long, hard look. The guy already had three sixes. Did he even know the rules of blackjack?

"Anything over twenty-one and you go bust, sir. Are you aware of that?"

Honeymoon guy looked blank, and Dex sighed. Clearly, the man had no clue.

Which, as the dealer, wasn't Dex's primary concern. His job was to maximize profits for the casino, which meant keeping the cards — and the money — flowing.

But, hell. The nervous bride peering over the groom's shoulder was just as young and clueless as her beau — and eight-plus months pregnant, judging by the baby bulge that practically screamed, *Here I come, world!* The few hundred dollars in chips the couple clutched were probably all they had, and Dex would be damned if they blew it on his watch.

He flashed Honeymoon Guy The Look.

You're done at this table, kid, Dex made sure his yellow-brown shifter eyes blazed. He would have liked to say, *Quit while you're ahead,* but it was more like *Quit before you lose even more.*

An order, not a suggestion, in other words.

Usually, that did the trick. Humans might be clueless about shifters, but few were dumb enough to miss a clear warning from an alpha male.

But Honeymoon Guy had looked down to check his cards — again — and missed the hint.

Dex rolled his eyes. How stupid could a human be?

There are better ways to earn money, kid, he wanted to say.

But dammit, that applied to him too. How the hell had he ended up dealing cards in a Las Vegas casino? A panther shifter like him ought to be prowling around the wilderness somewhere, breathing fresh air.

His inner beast rumbled, *Forget it. Let the guy lose.*

But he couldn't shake the image of that baby bump, so he growled under his breath.

Honeymoon Guy glanced around, wondering what the sound was. Then he tapped his cards. "I said, hit me."

Dex was tempted to hit him, all right — just not in the sense of dealing another card.

He turned on The Look again, socking the guy with his eyes.

"Um... Forget it. I changed my mind." Honeymoon Guy shrank back.

Dex hid a snort. That hadn't even been his most powerful glare — only as much as he dared to reveal, given the security guards and cameras scrutinizing him. A month had passed since his friend Tanner had pulled off the win of the decade at this very table, making off with two million dollars and a diamond worth even more.

Had Dex aided and abetted his friend? Hell yes. His share — a cool million in cash — was now stashed in a safe place.

Was he about to admit it? Hell no. Not to the band of bloodthirsty vampires who ran the casino. Let them think Tanner and his partner Karen had been operating on their own, as an investigation had already concluded.

Still, vampires were a suspicious bunch. Hence the heightened scrutiny of Dex's table.

Dex glanced at one of the many mirrors on the wall, confirming that his expression was as cool and collected as usual.

Being a panther helped — not that he let his animal side show other than in his powerful build. Just the usual him — short, buzz-cut hair and an equally short, boxed beard that outlined his dark skin in neat black lines. His black bow tie carried the look over to his work clothes — the crisp white shirt, black vest, and black pants. Not too shabby, in other words, and not the least bit suspicious.

Or so he hoped.

Still, he knew damn well that any lesser dealer would have long since been bumped off, guilty or not — or worse, fed to vampires who would suck him dry of every last drop of blood. But Dex was the casino's best dealer, and that was his ace. A worn-out ace that had been played a few too many times, if he had to admit it. He had to tread carefully, in other words, if he wanted to stay alive.

"Oh!" Bob, a regular, made a show of looking at his watch. "It's almost time for the two-for-one, all-you-can-eat brunch at Bloody Mary's."

Honeymoon Girl's eyes lit up, and she tugged on the groom's sleeve. "Finish up, honey. That sounds too good to miss."

Bob winked at Dex — a move the security cameras would surely catch. But as a hedgehog shifter, Bob had nothing to fear. Not when the vampires couldn't get past his quills. Dex, on the other hand. . .

Watch it, Dex rumbled into his friend's mind.

Bob grinned in a way that made him look more like Danny DeVito than ever. Small, a tad round, and crafty. *I'll make sure to lose the next few rounds.*

Dex called the round, and everyone leaned back with a sigh. One woman exceeded the dealer's hand of twenty, but everyone else lost.

"Hey!" Honeymoon Guy blurted as Dex reached for his chips. "Three sixes is three of a kind, right?"

"Wrong game, sir." Dex pointed to the poker tables. "Try there next time."

Bob pointed at his watch. "Only the first twenty customers get the two-for-one deal, you know."

ANNA LOWE

Honeymoon Girl grabbed her beau by the collar and
marched him toward the restaurant, where a gazelle shifter
hostess bounded over to greet them.

"Welcome to Bloody Mary's! Table for two?"

So, whew. At least that happy couple had been spared
further losses — for now.

And what about you? Bob murmured into Dex's mind.
Shouldn't you be long gone too?

Dex kept his face straight while dealing the next round of
cards. *Only a guilty man runs, and I have nothing to hide.*

Other than that million in cash, Bob's amused look said.

A damn good thing you could count on a hedgehog to keep
a secret.

Business was slow, and the next couple of rounds were the
easy, mindless kind. Enough that Dex's thoughts could stray
to his million bucks and everything he could do now that he
was rich.

Except, that's not where his thoughts went. Instead, they
drifted to the image of the woman he loved.

Dakota, his panther hummed, dreaming about the field of
freckles splattering her suntanned cheeks. How many kisses
would it take to touch each one?

With an effort, he forced his thoughts back to a less com-
plicated issue — his cash. What to do with a million dollars?

His first thought had been to buy a new car and a nice
house and finally live in style. Maybe a place back home in
Florida with a river view.

His second thought had been to steer clear of Tanner's crazy
plan and the trouble it was sure to bring. And, hell. He'd been
right.

If only his better angels hadn't intervened with the notion
of donating the money to his sister's Save the Florida Panther
foundation. And the more time passed, the more he liked the
idea. He'd always been a bit of a drifter, and that was okay.
But to make a difference — *really* make a difference — in a
good cause for his distant panther kin... That, he couldn't
resist.

4

The thing was, neither plan mattered if he didn't survive the next few weeks. One false move could land him on the short end of a straw filled with blood. His blood.

A shiver went down his spine.

Which brought him to Plan C — getting out of Vegas alive. Preferably with the money, but worst-case... Well, just alive.

But, as usual, his panther had a better plan.

Stay alive AND keep the money for the foundation AND win my mate.

Greedy bastard, in other words.

But just the thought of the latter made his soul sing.

Dakota... Dakota...

Simply rolling his tongue around her name sent butterflies fluttering around his heart, and the memory of their last, sizzling night together made his blood heat.

Dakota might be human, and she might not know that he was a shifter, but she was his mate. The first time they'd met, he'd stopped in his tracks, and his jaw had gone slack. His heart thumped to a whole new beat — a quick, jazzy one that told him life with her would be one long, beautiful improv full of joy and rewards.

If only he had processed that right away. Only now that he faced losing her did he finally understand what that new, skipping beat in his heart meant.

She's our destiny. Our future. Our everything, his panther hummed.

True love, he agreed. The kind that never faded and never brought regret.

He frowned. No regrets, except not being tuned in enough to realize how much she meant to him until now. Was it too late?

A movement caught his eye — one of the two security guards watching his table — and Dex's gut clenched. It was the guy with long, slicked-back hair, sunglasses, and skin so pale, it was practically translucent.

Vampire.

Cursing under his breath, Dex glanced over to the second guard, a bear shifter. Which was almost as bad, because bears had the best noses on earth, and that one was a stickler for reporting every little thing. If he somehow sensed Dakota's residual scent...

Bile rose in Dex's throat. The vampires could — and would — use Dakota as their own ace.

He could picture it now... Getting called into the head office, where Igor Schiller would flash his long, pointy fangs.

Perhaps we should go over last month's unfortunate incident one more time. Is there anything further you'd like to share about that day? It would be a pity if a certain Miss Starr met an ugly fate, don't you think?

He clenched his jaw. He had to keep Dakota out of this. Even if that meant losing her, he couldn't take the risk.

A dozen knives plunged into his heart and twisted at the same time. So far, he'd managed to go three weeks without seeing her. Without so much as sending her a message, in fact, because the vampires could trace his calls. Who knew what she thought of him now?

The deck of cards he was shuffling nearly flew out of his hands, and he cursed. But he had to stick with his plan, no matter how much it hurt. No matter how many hours he spent staring at the ceiling each night, yearning for his mate, or how slowly the minutes of his hollow, lonely life ticked by. He had to keep her safe.

His panther yowled. *Can't live without our mate.*

When he dealt the next hand, a customer turned over her first card, the queen of hearts.

The next card was the ace of spades — Dex's lucky card — and his hopes soared. But not long after, a king of hearts appeared — the suicide king with the sword through his head — and Dex frowned. Was that an omen?

He pushed the thought out of his mind. With any luck, he could lie low for a while, shake off the vampires, and then reunite with his mate.

But when? Where? How? Dakota had been planning to leave Vegas soon. For all he knew, she could already be gone.

Then again, no one planned to stay in Vegas long, but lots of folks ended up there for years. Like Bob, who still remembered when most of The Strip was open desert.

Dex's blood pressure rose as the security guard approached him with purposeful steps. The vampire tapped his watch, signaling break time. Then he turned to the guests.

"Ladies and gentlemen, we'll be closing this table after this round."

Dex flashed his best grin. "You all must be winning too much."

Everyone laughed. Anyone who'd been paying attention would know the opposite was true. But, hell. Hope sprung eternal, even in Sin City.

Minutes later, Dex wrapped up the round and stood with his customary bow.

"Ladies and gents, it's been a pleasure. Enjoy your stay at the Scarlet Palace." In his mind, Dex tacked on a silent, *Oh, and steer clear of vampires.*

With that, he headed for the bar, where Randy, the unicorn shifter bartender, was sporting his best Boy George look. He winked and ran a hand along the rim of his bowler hat. "What do you think? Be honest."

Dex accepted his usual on-duty drink, a ginger ale. "I would, but I wouldn't want to hurt you."

Randy split into chuckles and smacked Dex on the shoulder. "Good one."

With that, Randy turned to another customer, humming the first lines of the song.

A group of showgirls strutted by the opposite side of the bar like a flock of excited peacocks — or whatever those four-foot neon feathers were supposed to evoke.

"Heya, Dex," the one named Crystal called. "You doing good, hon?"

He raised his glass. "You bet. How about you?"

"Couldn't be better, baby. First show of the day, coming right up."

The showgirls waved and blew kisses. As they paraded past, the feathers formed a nearly continuous wall. Strangely, Dex felt a sudden wave of attraction, which didn't fit. Then one of the girls teetered on her six-inch heels, giving him a glimpse of the main entrance beyond.

Dex froze.

Correction — on the outside, he remained cool as a cat. But on the inside, his heart revved, and he stared. That shouldn't — couldn't — be possible.

The parade of feathers continued, and it was all he could do not to peer over, under, or around the showgirls for a second look. He was that desperate for a glimpse of that sandy blond hair, those no-nonsense eyes.

Dakota? Here?

Dakota! his inner panther cheered.

Finally, the showgirls moved on, and hot damn — there she was. Dakota. No wonder he'd felt a zing.

Her long, straight hair swung as she glanced around — with attitude, like a cowgirl on the hunt for a runaway bull. A fed-up cowgirl, low on patience, high on *Don't mess with me* sass. Tall and lanky, she wore jeans that weren't stonewashed, just thoroughly broken in. The same went for her boots — all function, not fashion accessory.

Her nose was a pretty little button — not that he'd ever dare put it that way — and her sharp eyes studied the crowd. Hazel eyes, a mesmerizing mix of green and brown. Unpredictable, yet irresistible, just like her.

And the moment those eyes landed on him, her mouth cracked open as if a live wire connected her heart to his.

Zap! His body shook with it too. That rush of love, lust, and hope he'd missed so much over the past few weeks.

"Dakota," he whispered.

Then his stomach lurched. Shit. What was she doing here?

He whipped his head away, but it was too late. Richard, the vampire, had followed his gaze. Now, the shithead was touching his ear and murmuring into his mouthpiece.

Dex's eyes went wide. If Richard got a good look at Dakota...

"Crystal! Brooke!" He rapped his knuckles on the bar. "How about a round of drinks on me? I mean, something healthy to start your day right." He dropped his voice. "Make it quick, Randy."

"Oh, Dex!" The showgirls cooed, blew more kisses, and flocked to the bar, blocking Richard's view of the door.

"Pineapple smoothie for me," Crystal started, and the others chimed in with their orders next.

Dex hustled around them, praying the feathers of their headdresses covered the cameras by the doors too.

"Dex, sweetheart." Another of the showgirls batted inch-long eyelashes. "How can we ever repay you?"

"No need." He rushed past.

The good news was, the showgirls had all but engulfed Dakota, keeping her out of sight. The bad news was they made it hard to work his way past, what with all those smooches and pats to his ass. When he finally made it over to Dakota, he was smeared with lipstick.

Dakota stuck her hands on her hips. "Sweetheart? Baby?"

He grabbed her by the elbow and hustled her out the door. "I swear, I'll explain. But right now, we have to get out of here."

Chapter Two

Dakota's feet scrambled for purchase as Dex half carried, half shoved her outside. The blinding sun and searing desert temperatures hit her like a physical force, but that was nothing compared to the heat in her cheeks. That was the heat of anger mixed with the heat of arousal because, dammit, Dex was doing it again — turning her on like a cat in heat.

"Hey!" The soles of her boots skidded along the sidewalk.

"You can't be here." Dex bustled her along.

She wrenched her arm free. "Nice to see you too."

He stuck up his hands. "It is nice to see you. No, it's great to see you. I missed you so much."

His voice cracked with yearning, and his expression changed. Ninety-nine percent of the time, Dex was as *cool* and *aloof* as could be. Charismatic, confident, in charge. She'd only ever seen the remaining one percent when they were alone. And that tiny fraction broke down into countless flavors, like the dreamy flutter of his eyelids whenever they kissed. The raw laughter when she cracked a joke. The wonder that made his cheeks shine whenever they were in bed.

But all that was in private. Now, he was out in broad daylight, exuding so much sorrow, she nearly felt bad.

Nearly. But, hell. Not after the past three weeks.

"You missed me so much you haven't called or returned a message in weeks? So much, the minute you see me, you shove me out the door?"

Dammit, her voice was getting shrill, and every time she shoved him, he stumbled back. But he deserved it, the jerk.

Or did he? His lips twitched with unspoken words, and his eyes begged.

Please, Dakota. Please, hear me out, those eyes said. Eyes like a harvest moon — dark as night but tinged with a golden hue.

Then he glanced over his shoulder, cursed, and shooed her toward the street.

"I'll explain. I swear. But it's not safe here."

She nearly laughed. Nothing about Vegas was safe, from man-made trouble to the brutal desert heat.

"Not safe?" She snorted. "I've jumped from one speeding car to another. I've stood bareback on a galloping horse. I've hung out of flying helicopters. Don't lecture me about being safe."

"Those were movie stunts." Dex towed her along. "And believe me, I'm your number one fan. But this is the real thing, Dakota. Real bad guys who won't hold back."

She stared. Dex actually looked... Well, not scared, because nothing scared him. More like... spooked. Spooked enough for her to glance over her shoulder too.

"What have you gotten yourself mixed up in?"

His face was grim. "Something I don't want you mixed up in." He glanced left, then cursed. "Cameras. Quick — move."

He hustled her into the bushes that fringed the casino's entrance. When he stopped and peered through the foliage, Dakota did too. Was Dex crazy, or was there really some foe out there? It was hard to tell, given the red-tinged fountains spurting away in front of the Scarlet Palace.

For a moment, they crouched shoulder-to-shoulder in the tight space between the bushes and the casino's outer wall. Then she put a hand on his arm.

"Dex..."

She meant to follow that up with, *Tell me what's going on. Now.* But the moment their eyes locked, her heart swelled, and little harps went off in her ears.

Which was crazy. The only men she allowed to sweep her off her feet were fellow stunt men when a script called for it. But even then, she could crush the guy's balls with a well-aimed kick or leap on a motorcycle to escape.

With Dex, on the other hand... Her girl parts all sighed at the same time, as if Cupid had just whacked her with a love arrow and sealed her fate.

It was just like the first time she'd met him, with time halting in its tracks and a thousand bells going off in her mind, like she'd hit Vegas's biggest jackpot and was about to cash in big. Not in money, maybe, but in love. Enough for a rich and happy future if only she heeded the primal call in her veins.

The one that whispered, *This man is the one.*

She gulped, and *What the hell is going on?* nearly turned into *I was so worried about you.*

A good thing her pride kicked in and turned that into, "What's going on?"

The question was only half aimed at whatever threat had Dex so spooked. The rest referred to the humming sensation that always seemed to swirl around them when they got close. The joyous chorus singing in her ears, the irresistible urge to nestle close. That powerless feeling that some greater force was meddling with her life — in a good way.

When he cupped her cheek, she closed her eyes and leaned in. In no time, dreamy images were dancing through her mind — some of the past, some of the future. The time she and Dex had gone dancing at a poky cowboy bar. The evening they'd driven way out into the desert to watch the sun set. The very first morning she'd woken up at his side, and the last one, not too long ago.

"Dex..." She forced her eyes open and traced the perfect line of his neatly trimmed beard.

He gave himself a shake, as if he had been equally checked out for a minute there. Then he went back to peering around like a soldier at the Alamo's last stand.

"I'll explain. I swear I will. But right now, you have to get out of here. I can't let them see you with me."

"Let who?"

His Adam's apple bobbed. "The more you know, the more dangerous it is for you."

She formed a fist in front of his face. "And the less you tell me, the more dangerous it will be for you."

His eyes went wide, but he pointed. "Look. There."

She shielded her eyes from the sun and spotted three security types running out of the casino entrance. The trio looked around, murmuring into earphone mics.

Dakota backed another inch into the bushes. "Whoa. What did you do?"

She patted his nearest pocket, half expecting to find a giant wad of cash. But there was nothing — just the edge of the casino ID card clipped to his belt.

His face twisted. "Nothing. Well, nothing they didn't have coming."

She stared.

"No time to explain now." Dex coiled his muscles, ready to spring into action. "Get ready. This could be your chance to escape."

She followed the jerk of his chin toward the dozen or so protesters converging on the entrance to the casino. Clad entirely in white, like some kind of überhygienic cult, they wielded big signs the way knights wielded swords.

"Stop the bloodsuckers!" one of the protesters yelled.

The others took up the rallying call. "Stop them before they bleed everyone dry."

Dakota stared. Wow. Those guys were really concerned about visitors losing money at the casino.

The security men blanched and jabbered urgently into their mics. Meanwhile, tourists yanked out phones and filmed the spectacle, forming a crowd.

"Go! Go!" Dex shoved her toward the street in a crouched jog.

"Stop the bloodsuckers!" a protester cried.

"Take the *Scarlet* out of the Palace!" another yelled.

"Eat vegan!" a third chipped in.

Dakota snorted as she ran. "Kind of a broad agenda, don't you think?"

Dex's eyes darkened, and she swore he muttered, "If only you knew."

But it was hard to be sure, what with the increasing commotion and the leaves smacking against her body, now that Dex was pushing her through another hedge.

"How did you get here?" he asked.

She made a face. Did she really want to admit to spending another day combing through casinos for the missing lover she was worried sick about?

Definitely not.

"Um... I left my pickup at the Bellagio and walked from there."

Dex stared at her, then down the miles-long Strip, shimmering in the midday heat.

She stuck her hands on her hips. "What?"

Just then, a city bus rolled into a nearby stop, and Dex rushed her toward it. "Take that and get away. Far away. I finish work at five. Then I'll come to you. I promise."

She dug in her heels. "What happened to dangerous? For you, I mean."

Dex shook his head. "I need to finish my shift so they don't suspect anything. Then I'll make sure I'm not followed on my way over."

If he hadn't looked so goddamned earnest, she would have questioned him. But the bus doors opened with a hiss, and air-conditioned air blasted her face.

"But—"

Dex sent her into the bus with an insistent nudge.

"I swear, I'll come to you." With him down on the sidewalk and her two steps up, he looked like a knight taking a vow on his knees. "Name the place and time. I'll be there. I swear."

She hesitated, then gave in. "Hot Shots." His expression was blank, so she added, "The gun range. You know it?"

"I'll find it."

She folded her arms tightly. "Six o'clock tonight. Don't be late."

Dex opened his mouth to reply, but the doors slid shut just then. In the end, all she caught was a tiny nod as his lips shaped the words, *Hot Shots. At six.*

Chapter Three

Never had a couple of hours dragged by so slowly, only to speed up again. Business at Hot Shots always picked up in the evenings, and a mix-up in reservations didn't help.

Dakota cursed. Why had she ever accepted a half share of a shooting range in lieu of payment for a job? And dammit, why had she told Dex six?

As for the shooting range... Well, she hadn't had much choice when a film company she'd worked for had gone bankrupt. And as for Dex...

She frowned. For all she knew, he might not even show up. He might *never* show up.

Her heart ached the way it had over the past three agonizing weeks. Which stung doubly, because she'd never been the kind to pine for a man. Any man.

But then Dex had come along and rocked her world.

"Um, Dakota..." Wayne, one of her employees, shifted from foot to foot.

She forced her focus back to the reservations list. The bachelor party was insisting they had booked for six, but she had them down for eight. Meanwhile, the Henderson party had also arrived.

Stepping from her office to the lobby, Dakota could instantly tell which group was which. The ten guys with guts that were starting to outgrow their faded fraternity shirts were the bachelor party, while the seven women glaring at them had to be the ones booked for a *Sayonara, Baby* package. A divorce party, in other words.

A woman with a severe haircut and matching expression stuck her hand up. "We were here first."

"Lighten up, lady," one of the frat boys muttered.

"God, you sound like my ex," she snipped.

"The jerk," one of her friends threw in.

Dakota stepped forward. "No problem. Right this way, ladies. Have you brought your own targets today?"

The first woman grinned and held up a marriage certificate. "Sure did."

"Oh, and this." Her friend handed over a scrolled-up sheet with a giant pink bow. "We had it made for you, Violet."

The woman unrolled it and cackled in glee. "Oh, this is perfect."

The men shuffled back at the sight of it: a full-body image of a man photoshopped out of a wedding photo — Violet's ex, no doubt — with a bull's-eye centered on his groin.

Behind the wincing bachelors, the lobby door opened, and Dex slipped in, as stealthy as a thief. A very appealing, very sexy one. The thief of her heart?

Dakota puffed a breath of air upward. God, she hated the way her heart went pitter-patter at the sight of him. But he lit up too, and when their eyes locked, time stood still.

A good thing Wayne nudged her then.

"Um... Perfect," Dakota tried to remember where she'd left off.

He's perfect, all right, her inner vixen said.

Then again, that was probably what Violet had once thought of her ex.

Dakota shooed the divorce party to the right. "Wayne, get the ladies set up."

Wayne nodded. "One pink AK-47 coming right up. Or do you ladies prefer to start with the Glock?"

Violet flashed a vengeful glare at the likeness of her ex. "Both."

And off the divorce party went, fluttering with excitement.

Dakota turned to the bachelor party. The sooner she had those guys set up, the sooner she could talk to Dex.

"Darell, can you set up our other guests?"

She half turned away, then turned back, and hollered down the hallway. "Darell!"

A tattooed figure appeared from the storeroom, chewing on a toothpick. "Yes, boss?"

God, she hated his condescending tone. "Get these guys started on range four." *Now,* she nearly growled.

One of these days. . . her mind started.

She sighed. One of these days, she would unload her share of this business and get the hell out of Dodge. Then she could get back to doing honest work on a ranch, as she'd done before the film industry had lured her away. But for now. . .

She resisted the urge to hurry Darell along with a kick. "Have a good time, boys."

Half of the bachelor party looked delighted to be assigned a man's man like Darell, while the other half looked downcast.

"You're not coming, sweetheart?"

She nearly snorted. Yes, she was in her work outfit — a much-too-sexy, black leather bodysuit — but no, she was not about to encourage any fantasies they might harbor.

"You were in that movie, right?" one of the guys started. "What's it called. . ."

His buddy pointed to one of the movie posters on the wall. "*The Rough and the Ruthless.* I loved that one."

Dex followed his gaze, and Dakota winced. Of course, she'd mentioned her side job/turned stellar career/turned *Get me out of this warped Hollywood world.* But somehow, letting Dex see the PR images felt wrong. The drama, the spectacle — none of that was the real her.

"Just the stunts," she muttered.

"Those were the best part." The newest member of her fan club grinned.

"Wow. You were in all those movies?" another guy gushed.

She hid a sigh. "Yep."

The posters were Wayne's idea — anything to pull customers in and make Hot Shots memorable. Dakota had only agreed in hopes that any increased business might help her sell her share of the joint. But she'd been hoping for four months now without a single offer worth her time.

"Wow, even *Cowboy Avenger,*" one of the men raved. "Was that you jumping from horse to horse?"

"Yeah." She pointed sternly down the hall. "Now don't be late."

The guy's jaw dropped. "You look just like the warrior princess Khloe Maxx when you do that."

Dakota rolled her eyes. Apparently, he'd seen *Planet of Death.*

"Go," she barked.

He cringed and hurried after Darell.

"You tell him, honey." The last straggler of the divorce party gave her a little fist pump.

Dakota took a deep breath. "Thanks. Have fun."

For the next minute, the hall rang with the footsteps and chatter of excited guests. Then one heavy door after another slammed shut — in Violet's case, doubly hard — and sweet silence set in.

Dakota slumped back against the reception desk. God, what a day.

And now this. Slowly, she met Dex's gaze.

"Hi," he whispered after another few seconds ticked by.

"Hi."

Dakota swallowed against her too-dry throat. All her life, she'd worked with cool, composed men like him. Guys who held their cards close to their chests, like the wranglers on the ranch she'd grown up on or stunt men who pretended they didn't feel pain. And not one had ever affected her in any way.

But, damn. One look from Dex, and her cheeks burned. One word, and her soul danced. One touch, and she shivered in anticipation of more.

She stood a little taller and crossed her arms, remembering she was mad at him.

"So, I finally get to see where you work," Dex murmured.

When she shrugged, her ponytail caught on the zipper of her leather outfit. She tugged at her collar. "God, I hate this thing. It makes me feel like goddamn Catwoman."

Dex's eyes flashed the way they had when the two of them were alone and slowly, sensually stripping off layers of clothes.

"I hate my work clothes too."

20

She might have chuckled — except for the reminder of what had transpired earlier that day.

"Of all the places for you to work, I would never have guessed the Scarlet Palace."

He bit his lip. "Yes, about that..."

And just like that, her anger bubbled up again. All those days she'd spent worrying, searching...

"About that? About *that?*" Her voice rose. "What exactly is *that?*"

Memories flashed through her mind, from their first, chance meeting on a wilderness trail to the pizza dinner they'd shared afterward to their first kiss... Their first, unforgettable night together, and all the sizzling hours they'd spent in each other's arms since.

Not just that, but the hikes. The easy talks. The quiet, contemplative sunsets spent far from the glitz of Las Vegas. The little things that said it wasn't just about great sex.

But just when she'd been sure Dex was the real deal, he'd disappeared.

"I meant to get in touch," he tried.

"And yet, you didn't."

"I couldn't. I swear, I wanted to. But—"

"Couldn't or wouldn't?" She stabbed at his chest with her finger. "You disappeared off the face of the earth. I was worried." *Really worried,* she nearly admitted. "Then I was mad. *Really* mad."

Bang! Bang! Bang! The sharp crack of a Glock from the divorce party side of the gun range underscored her point.

"You have every right to be mad," Dex agreed. "But I had to lay low for a while. I was worried what they might do to you to get to me."

Rat-a-tat-tat-tat! Machine-gun fire broke out from the bachelor party side.

She arched an eyebrow. "Who is they?"

He shuffled closer, whispering, "The Scarlet Palace."

She studied his eyes, but there was no trace of a lie.

"And what would anyone suspect you of?"

21

Other than sinfully good looks and a smile that could melt a girl's panties, of course.

Under normal circumstances, Dex would have flashed a *Who, me?* grin, reinforcing her point. But his cheek twitched, and his eyes hit the floor as if he had something to hide.

Which didn't make sense. Dex was as honest and straight-up as they came. Painfully honest, almost. Plus, he moved like a mix between a prizefighter and a cat. A really big, really confident cat, like a tiger armed with claws and teeth. What had him so thrown?

When his eyes met hers with a look that said, *You,* her mouth fell open a crack.

She pursed her lips. So far, she'd only considered how worried she'd been about him. Had he been just as worried about her?

"What happened, Dex?"

He spoke in stops and starts. "You remember my friend Tanner? He needed money — for a good cause, I swear — so he arranged to... Um..."

A door on the left flew open, and one of the bachelors came stumbling out with an M4. "Uh, miss? Darell said to ask you about the crosshairs on this thing."

He fumbled awkwardly with the weapon, pointing it first at Dex, then at the door, then the bar.

"Whoa." Dakota grabbed the muzzle and jerked it toward the floor. "Didn't Darell teach you lesson one?"

The guy scratched his head. "Uh... Have fun?"

She rolled her eyes. "Safety first. Always keep the muzzle down. Always. Got it?"

"Got it." The minute he said it, the muzzle started drifting upward again.

Dakota shoved it back down. A damn good thing it was only loaded with pellets. But even those could cause permanent damage. "What's the problem?"

"It keeps missing."

She rolled her eyes and refrained from saying, *You keep missing, moron.*

Instead, she tapped on the crosshairs adjuster. "You'll have to experiment with this. Okay?"

Teaching kindergarten would be easier, she figured.

"Go on, try it." She shooed him back toward the range. Once he'd gone, she hissed at Dex. "Don't give me that look."

He stuck up his hands. "What look?"

She pointed at him. "That one."

A cheer went up from range three as an earsplitting ping sounded.

Dex winced. "Was that the wedding ring?"

Dakota shrugged. "Not all men keep their promises, you know."

Dex's throat bobbed, and a shadow of shame passed over his eyes.

"Tanner and his girlfriend staged a diversion at the casino and made off with a couple million bucks," he finally continued. "Not that they stole it — they won it fair and square. But they disabled the early warning systems so the managers couldn't come play their usual tricks to break up a winning streak. The management was really pissed off, and since I was the dealer at that table..."

Her eyes narrowed. She'd never thought Dex was the type to get mixed up in such things. But maybe she was wrong. Maybe he was a con man and the only thing he wasn't lying about was the importance of steering clear of him.

"And your role in this was...?"

"Um... I might have helped disable the alarm." He tried a weak grin. "Oh, and timed it so the fewest guards were on duty. And I might also have—"

She stuck up a hand. "Maybe I don't want to hear this."

"That's what I mean. The more you know, the more danger you could be in. That's why I had to stay away."

"And yet, here you are."

"You told me to come."

She crossed her arms. "I'm starting to regret that."

His face barely flickered, but his eyes turned as sad as a puppy's.

23

Dakota gulped and lowered her voice. "Sorry. I didn't mean that. But please — just explain. Maybe I can help."

Hope trickled back into Dex's eyes, and she couldn't hold back a tiny smile. There it was again — a hint of that hidden one percent. The fraction no one but she glimpsed.

But instead of explaining, Dex gazed silently into her eyes. Then he opened his arms, and just like that, they were wrapped in a hug. Much like their first night together, it just happened, all by itself, the way fall snuck up on summer and winter snuck up on fall. It was that natural, that unstoppable.

She closed her eyes and inhaled his fresh, woodsy scent. God, she'd missed him.

The way his arms tightened around her said the same thing.

"Believe me, I never wanted to leave," he whispered, stroking her hair. "I just need to figure some way out of this mess."

"So, talk to me. Let me help."

But just as Dex pulled away and took a deep breath, about to speak, cheers and gunfire exploded from the divorce party's firing range.

Wayne popped his head out the door. "Uh, Dakota? They're not listening."

She cursed and eased away from Dex. "Maybe this isn't the best time or place."

"When, then?"

Her step hitched as her sensible side piped up, saying, *If he's in trouble, you need to keep away.*

Her heart ached. Sure, but this was Dex. How could she not hear him out? How could she not help?

Then again, she'd made bad choices in the past. Like her first boyfriend — self-centered bastard that he'd turned out to be — and her second, a guy nearly twice her age. Then there was that irresistibly charismatic stunt man she'd briefly hooked up with... Key word for that one: brief. Worst of all was that bullshitter of a leading man she'd nearly fallen for. What had she ever seen in him?

She pinched her lips. For a woman who could pull off just about any stunt, she had a pretty dismal record when it came to men.

Dex is different, a voice resonated deep in her bones. *Dex is the one.*

Her throat was so dry, it hurt to swallow. Should she give him one more chance or cut him off there and then?

Dex's eyes pleaded with her — not to give him another chance, but to reject him — for her own sake.

"Tomorrow night," she finally said. "Sunset. Out at Painted Rock."

His eyes shone. *Painted Rock, our special place?*

She nodded quickly, before any doubt could set in.

"See you then."

Chapter Four

Dex pulled into the trailhead parking lot and cruised to a stop. There was no sign of Dakota's pickup, which meant either meant he was early or...

His heart pounded faster as he jumped out of his classic Camaro and looked around. What if something had happened to her?

He sniffed the air hurriedly as his inner panther lashed its tail. No hint of Dakota. He jumped onto a boulder, scrutinizing every vehicle that rushed along the distant highway. Seconds later, he checked his phone. Dammit, where was she?

The sky was streaked with yellow-orange light, making the jagged mountains look redder than ever. The earth underfoot radiated dry heat, while the air temperature cooled quickly. The perfect time for a panther to slink off into the wild and explore...

...or to pace around a parking lot and fret.

He cursed himself for agreeing to this remote meeting point, but what could he do? He couldn't risk meeting Dakota at his place, because it had been ransacked — twice. As if he were fool enough to stash his loot there.

No, out here made more sense. It was far enough for him to make sure he hadn't been followed and wild enough to feel like home turf.

Still, his nerves remained on edge. Every pickup that appeared in the distance raised, then shattered, his hopes. He took three steps back toward his car, only to about-face and keep a lookout again. Shoot. He would give anything to go back to the carefree lifestyle he'd led until a few weeks ago. Back then, he would have enjoyed the last rays of sunshine without the slightest worry, confident that Dakota would arrive safe and sound. But now...

Anything? a little voice whispered in his mind. *You would truly give anything?*

He nodded. Anything.

Even a million dollars?

He nodded immediately. Of course.

Then he blinked at the setting sun, pondering that revelation. One that had been sneaking up on him over weeks, though he'd only wised up to it recently. A date here, a hike there, leading to the first of many nights of ecstasy. Then there were the blissful mornings-after that left them both with smiles that lasted most of the day — smiles that revived the moment they saw each other again. All that happy humming he'd been doing lately. All that joy. All those hopes and dreams suddenly populating his mind.

All that wasn't just a lucky streak. It was destiny.

She was his destiny.

He rubbed both hands over his cheeks. His mother had always said he failed to see the forest for the trees. But damn. To be so slow in recognizing his mate?

Then again, panthers weren't like bears, wolves, or any of those species that were so big on fated mates. Like most felines, panthers tended to feel pretty satisfied on their own. Who needed a mate?

Until that miraculous day came — if you were lucky enough — and you saw the light.

His panther lashed its tail from side to side. *Mate.*

At the sound of tires crunching over gravel, Dex whipped his head up just in time to see Dakota coast into the parking lot with a wave.

"Sorry I'm late."

His mouth opened and closed, though no sound came out. And hell, what would he say?

Actually, I'm the one who's late. Painfully late in realizing the obvious.

As Dakota cruised by on her way to a parking spot, his chest lifted and filled. Man, was the air crisp and cool. And, wow, was the sky beautifully clear.

She jumped down from the cab, shouldering a backpack. "Hey."

Her long, loose hair swung with her usual, unstoppable momentum, and her freckled cheeks rounded as she flashed a tight smile.

He swallowed the lump in his throat. "Hey."

The first few steps they took toward each other were measured and calm. The next few were a little faster, and the final few. . .

They crashed into a hug and hung on.

He stroked her back, shielding her from the dangers of the outside world and refusing to let go. Thinking about that *anything* he'd been considering before.

Anything, he decided. Everything. He would give everything for her.

"Let's get out of here," he whispered.

Dakota laughed and turned toward the trailhead. "Sure."

He grabbed her hand and motioned toward his car. Her car. Hell, any car.

"No, I mean, let's get out of Vegas. Now. Just hop in the car and go. Leave all this shit behind and start new somewhere else."

She stared.

That's a yes, his panther decided, and he started tugging her toward the car.

"Whoa. Wait." She dug her heels in. "Now?"

"What's holding us back?"

"Um. . . My job. Your job. . . "

"I hate mine. You hate yours. You said you wanted to leave."

"When I've sold my share in the business."

He shook his head. "Not worth the risk."

Her eyes narrowed. Beautiful hazel eyes like moss growing by a riverbank.

29

"Right, the risk. Something you were going to tell me about... when?"

He tilted his head toward the highway. "I can tell you on the way."

She stood her ground. "No, you can tell me right here."

A dog came running down the trailhead, followed by a family of four, and Dakota corrected herself. "Make that, at Painted Rock. Let's go." And off she charged, waving to the family as they passed. "Nice views?"

"Great," they gushed.

Soon, Dakota's long legs had her bounding up the trail and scrambling over rocks so quickly, it was all he could do to keep up. She trotted through a grove of ash trees where they startled a feral burro, then wound noiselessly along a sandstone canyon, barely leaving a footprint in the sand.

She would make a great panther, his animal side hummed.

Yes, she would. And damn, did the woman have a sense of direction, heading straight for the secluded place they'd found weeks ago and dubbed Painted Rock. All at a pace that said she was challenging the sun to a race of who could reach their destination first — the sun slipping below the horizon or Dakota reaching Painted Rock.

"Almost there," she murmured when they passed a hidden spring.

Your average person would have considered that the finish line, because Painted Rock reared high on the right. But Dakota scurried up the steep slope as nimbly as a mountain goat.

A panther, his inner beast insisted.

Part of him yearned to shift and reveal his inner feline to her then and there. He would pad smoothly over the scrubby terrain and pass her within a few steps. Then he would leap from one rocky outcrop to another, showing her how great life as a shifter could be.

Dakota would love it, he was sure. There was just the little issue of explaining the shifter world... Fated mates... Mating bites... The vampires he had to avoid...

His shoulders slumped. Where to begin? How? As a human, Dakota had no clue about such things.

"Hurry up," she called over her shoulder. "The sun is about to set."

When he finally caught up, her cheeks had a triumphant glow that mirrored the color of the western horizon. She held up her water bottle in a silent toast, chugged down several gulps, then took a deep breath that declared, *Mission accomplished. Now, on to my next feat...*

The problem was, the next feat was up to him. Namely, explaining what was going on.

The summit of Painted Rock was smooth and wide enough to hold a dozen hikers, though they were the only two in sight. Just him, her, and the stars, emerging one by one in the endless indigo sky.

Dakota plonked down and patted the space next to her. "You're procrastinating."

He couldn't help but smile. They'd only met six weeks earlier, yet she knew him better than he knew himself.

"Come on. Out with it." Dakota nudged him. "The truth, the whole truth, and nothing but the truth."

Sitting beside her, he took a deep breath and finally began. With the truth, if not the whole truth, because he couldn't bring himself to explain the vampires or shifter part — yet.

"My friend Tanner came to Las Vegas to beat the casino owners at their own game — all for a good cause. They were planning to build a new casino in a wilderness area near Tanner's home..."

Tanner's den was more like it, because the man was a bear shifter. But Dex left that part out.

"His girlfriend Karen helped..."

Tanner's girlfriend, who has half dragon, half witch. Dex skipped that part too, emphasizing what a just cause it was and how, technically, they hadn't broken any rules. No counting cards, no hidden aces. They had simply made sure security wasn't alerted when Karen started winning big and kept it up for hand after lucky hand.

31

"I had a good cause, too," he added. "Save the Florida Panther. Do you know how quickly their numbers are dwindling? And a lot of that is preventable, because so many are killed on roads. But if we build more wildlife underpasses and establish natural corridors..."

He started getting carried away there, having had a few close shaves himself back home. And that was as a shifter, who ought to know enough about the human world to avoid such things. Wild panthers, on the other hand, didn't have a chance, and with the way their habitat was continually reduced...

Oops. Definitely getting carried away. He forced himself back to the point. "Did you see the showgirls at the casino yesterday?"

Dakota made a face. "How could I miss them? All those sequins, all that bare skin."

"All those feathers, blocking the security cameras." Dex stuck up an arm, mimicking the headdresses.

Dakota cracked up. "Seriously? That worked?"

"Yes — oh, and I might have snipped one little wire so the warning signal didn't reach the surveillance guys. But it was corroded anyway."

"I bet," Dakota muttered dryly.

"It was!"

Still, she kept up that *not amused* look, and he chuckled. "That guy was right."

Her brow furrowed. "What guy?"

"The one at the shooting range. You really do look like that warrior princess when you do that."

"I only did the stunts."

He grinned. "Those were the best part."

She swatted his arm. "Quit changing the subject. What happened next?"

He shrugged. "Tanner and Karen took off with the winnings and wired me my share. Even though there was no evidence I was involved, the casino has been keeping a close eye on me. That's why I stayed away, Dakota. These guys are big-time crooks. Not the kind you mess with."

He nearly added, *Especially since they can sprout fangs and suck your blood.*

"What, like some kind of mafia?"

"Worse."

"What's worse than the mafia?"

"Guys who enjoy killing. Who love blood."

She drew back, but he went on, making his point.

"Guys I swear can see through me sometimes. Like Lucifer reborn. Like... like... creatures of the night." He stuck up a hand. "I know it sounds nuts, but that's what they're like. They'll stop at nothing. They forgive nothing."

Her throat bobbed. "But they haven't touched you, right?"

"So far, no. Not as long as I make them good money, at least."

She flashed a little smile. "Too charming for your own good, huh? Bringing in the customers and keeping them there?"

He shrugged. Pretty much, he supposed.

Dakota poked him. "You honestly didn't think they would watch you?"

"I guess I wasn't too worried about it. Not when they had no evidence and nothing to hold over me. But then..."

He hesitated, gazing out over the vastness of the desert. The undulating bedrock, the muted reds and browns. The air so dry, a whisper could carry a mile.

He cleared his throat and finally got it out. "But then I realized there was something. No, someone. Someone I cared about enough for them to use against me."

His breath caught, because they'd never gotten around to a conversation like this before. Hell, they'd never thought too far into the future or uttered the L word. They'd been having too much fun in the present to think ahead to all that. But now...

Funny how one stupid stunt could make so many things clear.

Dakota's shoulder was touching his, and she was just as still as he. So was the desert, waiting for him to man up enough to say it out loud.

"Someone you care about, huh?" Dakota whispered.

He nodded, then clasped her hand with both of his. A lot like the way his mother used to clutch her Bible on Sundays when she knelt in the church pews. And, hell. Maybe this was his pew, and the stars his spiritual guides.

"You know how it goes," he said in a scratchy voice. "How you never know how much something means to you until it's too late?"

With that, he kissed her hand. A laughably chaste gesture, considering all the times they'd laid each other bare and indulged in wild fantasies. But somehow, it seemed more intimate than anything they'd ever done before.

"Someone I love," he finally managed.

The breeze was light, and there were only a few scraps of grass around to be stirred, but to Dex, it seemed as if the whole universe was thundering with applause.

Dakota curled her fingers around his and leaned in.

"Love, huh?"

He nodded. "Love. It took me a while to figure that out, though." He dug a foot into the ground. "But I'm not sure she feels the same."

She stroked the back of his hand with her thumb, chewing over her words. "She does. I mean. . . " She cleared her throat. "I do."

His heart soared like a kite.

Her fingers tightened around his. "And you might not be the only one who didn't realize what you had." She stopped long enough to gulp hard, then whispered, "But you know what?"

He turned, coming face-to-face. "What?"

A bird could have fluttered by and been quieter than his voice just then, and he cursed himself.

But Dakota must have caught it, because she went on. "It might not be too late."

He moved his mouth to reply, but somehow, it ended up as a kiss instead. A kiss as light as a feather, yet it rocked his soul.

She slid a hand over his shoulder and around his back, nestling closer.

34

"Definitely not too late," she whispered. "After all, here we are."

Dex shifted around, giving her space to press in. "Here we are."

She nodded solemnly, slowly pressing him back to lie on the smooth rock. The very rock they'd made love on a few times in the past.

Dex caught the thought there and corrected himself. Maybe that hadn't been making love so much as just plain sex. But he vowed that what was about to happen would qualify for that loftier category.

When she straddled him, he ran his hands along her ribs, working her shirt up. But the thinking part of his mind made him pause. There was so much they had to discuss...

"Maybe we should—"

She shook her head. "Talk? Yes. Later. Right now..."

Maybe she had a point. Talking wasn't the only way to communicate. And they were both better at expressing themselves through deeds.

Dakota reared back, raising one eyebrow. "Any objections, mister?"

He shook his head. "No, ma'am."

She grinned and pulled her shirt off, followed by her bra. "Good, because you seem to have gotten me sidetracked again."

It's not me, he wanted to say. *It's destiny. I didn't realize it before. But now, I know.*

But there was no time, not with her coming back down for a deep, hungry kiss.

He grinned. With any other woman, he might be the one making those moves. But there was no other woman — none that had ever moved him the way this one did. And, heck. Dakota wouldn't be Dakota if she didn't know exactly what she wanted.

Knows what we want too, his panther hummed as she helped him work down his pants.

That, she did. And when they finally worked the rest of their layers off—

Dakota straddled him and slid down slowly, taking him in one scorchingly hot inch at a time. Then she tipped her head back and started rocking. Slowly at first, then faster. Faster...

Dex gripped her hips, gazing up at her and the stars. A view that grew hazier the more he thrust upward and the more Dakota cried out. But one thing remained perfectly, unwaveringly clear.

Mate, his panther hummed again and again. *Mate.*

There was no way he was leaving Vegas soon — not without her. But he would leave the details for later, because right now...

"Yes," Dakota moaned, rocking faster... Faster... Begging for more.

More, he was ready to give her, and not just tonight.

Chapter Five

Dakota splashed water on her face and studied herself in the bathroom mirror of her office at Hot Shots. Dammit, it had happened again. The previous evening, she'd let Dex's mesmerizing voice... eyes... touch — hell, his everything — carry her away into a dream world. Instead of sorting out their predicament, they'd ended up indulging in three sizzling rounds of sex, each hungrier and more primal than the previous one.

Not that she was complaining. It was just that she'd lost her sense of balance again. Somehow, that always happened around Dex.

Afterward, he'd urged her to leave Vegas with him, but she had come to her senses by then. Why? Because the casino owners wouldn't let city limits stop them if they wanted to target Dex.

Secondly, she was still processing her emotions. Yes, she loved Dex. Three frantic weeks without him had made that abundantly clear. But leaving Vegas to start a new life together was a big decision under normal circumstances. Doing so as a crime boss's target was an entirely different thing.

So, no. She wasn't going to turn tail and run blindly. Like any good stunt, their exit from Vegas had to be meticulously planned. That meant figuring out exactly where they stood. Maybe Dex was wrong about the casino's suspicions. Maybe if he lay low for long enough, he could leave Vegas without any trouble at all.

She frowned. How likely was that?

And third, she really wasn't comfortable with the way that money had been won, even if it had been for a good cause.

The way Dex spoke about panthers and the environment was a surprise. She knew he loved nature and the outdoors, but yikes. For relaxed, easy-going Dex to show that much passion and drive was really something.

Why panthers, in particular? she'd asked on the hike back.

Dex had hemmed, hawed, and finally mumbled something about being true to his roots in Florida. But somehow, that didn't seem like the full truth.

She splashed her face again. If only Dex hadn't drawn the ire of ruthless casino bosses in the process. But that was Dex — a little impulsive, a lot of heart, and not very big on planning ahead.

She, on the other hand, had long since had a plan. A good one. All that money she'd saved in the movie business... all those close calls pulling off iffy stunts... All that had been aimed at her own cause. After five years of stunt work and four months in Vegas, she was ready to get back to her own roots by buying a small ranch and living a quiet, honest, outdoorsy life.

The question was, how would Dex fit into that plan?

A knock sounded on the office door, pulling Dakota out of her reverie.

She stepped back into the office. "Come in."

Sweat glistened at Wayne's brow when he stuck his head in. "Your appointment is here."

She sighed and looked out the window. Nine p.m. Who the hell called a business meeting after dark? Then again, if the man who'd called earlier was serious about buying her share of the gun range, the sooner they met, the better.

"Great. Send him in."

Wayne slid the rest of the way into her office and closed the door. "I'm not sure you want to meet these guys. They're creepy."

She snorted. "At least half the Hollywood directors I've worked with were creeps. I can handle it."

Still, Wayne hesitated. "Super creepy. They remind me of the bad guys in *Spartacus Revamped*."

She rolled her eyes. "That was a movie, Wayne."

A pretty bad movie, to be honest. *Gladiators with a vampire twist,* her agent had laughed. *But, hell. They're offering double what you got for your last job.*

Wayne put a shaky hand on the doorknob. "Okay. But don't go asking me to bring coffee to your Transylvanian guests, boss."

He stepped out, leaving the door open. As voices drifted in from the lobby, Dakota cast a quick, longing glance at the postcard she'd pinned to a noticeboard. If this deal went well, she could head back to the mountains soon. Instead of the asphalt and pollution of Vegas, she would be inhaling fresh, pine forest air and marveling at Rocky Mountain vistas on horseback.

"Miss Starr," a brandy-smooth, accented voice sounded from the doorway.

"That's me. Come on in."

She spoke out of habit, then immediately regretted it. Wayne was right. The man — and the three behind with him — were downright creepy.

Each wore a tailored black suit over a black shirt and dark sunglasses — at night. Their dark, shiny hair was greased back in a limp, lifeless look. The only splash of color among any of them was the red handkerchief folded neatly into the first man's breast pocket.

Blood red, she decided.

Otherwise, three of the four looked alike — tall, lean, and pale. Really pale, like they never ventured out in the sun.

Dakota's cheek twitched. The fourth guy — the big, burly one with the sloppy tie — looked a hell of a lot like the security guard who had come running out of the Scarlet Palace after Dex had hustled her out.

"Mr. Schiller. Have a seat."

Without offering her hand, she lowered herself to her chair — a big leather one that screamed, *I'm the boss.*

"Please, call me Igor." His accent matched his looks. Russian? Bulgarian?

Transylvanian, Wayne mouthed from outside.

Two of the three men remained outside the office door, while the third closed it and stood towering behind Schiller. Bodyguards, in other words.

Schiller templed his fingers under his chin. "Let's get right to business, Miss Starr."

She nearly corrected him. Morgenstern was her real name, but for once, she didn't mind concealing that. Just in case.

"Yes. Let's. I understand you're interested in buying my share of Hot Shots?"

"Indeed. We at Scarlet Enterprises are in a growth phase and therefore are interested in expanding from the casino business to other branches of leisure."

Dakota went very, very still. This guy was from the Scarlet Palace?

"I see." She did her best not to fidget. That had to be a coincidence, right?

But, shit. Schiller's gaze was cold, unblinking. Reptilian, almost.

Guys I swear can see through me sometimes, Dex had said.

Yikes. Now Dakota knew what he meant.

"Hot Shots would be a great investment," Dakota added quickly. "Would you like to tour the premises or look at the numbers first?"

"The numbers, please."

She pulled up the first of several charts she'd prepared earlier that day.

"As you can see, business has been increasing steadily, especially over the past few months..."

"Ever since you joined the establishment, from what I understand." Schiller flashed a crocodile smile at her look of surprise. "I have done my homework, my dear."

Her nerves had already been on edge. Now, her stomach joined in, making her feel sick. What else did Schiller know?

She clicked, adding a new line to her chart. Anything to keep Schiller's focus on the business and not on her.

"This line shows the average industry profit margin, and this line above it represents Hot Shots. And on this next slide, you'll see our capital investments and expenses..."

Schiller's eyes stayed on hers, not all that interested. And, yikes. His gaze kept coming to rest on her neck. Or was that her pulsing jugular?

She gave herself a little shake. God, she could kill Wayne for putting that vampire imagery in her head.

Next, she hurried through demographics and on to revenue streams.

"One direction we're moving in is to diversify both. Our *Just Married* and *Sayonara, Baby* packages reflect that, and both have been a huge success."

"And what exactly do you have planned next?" Schiller watched her closely.

Dakota gripped her armrests, assuring herself he meant the business, not Dex, his million dollars, or getting out of Vegas alive.

"Training courses, for one thing — repackaged into short modules aimed at a transient customer base. VIP perks are also in the works, as well as strategic partnerships."

"Such as with us," Schiller pointed out.

Over my dead body, she nearly blurted, but why tempt fate?

"Exactly." She forced herself to smile. It came out all fake, but hell. So was Schiller.

"However, one area we never economize on is safety and security."

"Just like a casino," Schiller said in that hypnotizing, *I know something you don't know* voice. "I can assure you, we are very thorough."

"I imagine you must be." She flashed another smile so fake, it hurt her cheeks. Then she stood. "How about a tour of the premises?"

Schiller didn't seem particularly interested, but he went along.

Dakota's path out of the office took her directly past the big, burly bodyguard. And, shit. She could have sworn his nostrils flared as she swept by.

Shit, shit, shit. Had he recognized her, or was paranoia making her imagine the worst?

She hurried down the hallway, motioning left and right.

41

"The original ten lanes are here, and down this way, we added three separate, private lanes."

Darell was running another bachelor party in one, judging by the continuous stream of machine-gun fire and cheers.

"Of course, we do our best to sensitize customers to the seriousness of handling firearms," she went on.

A losing prospect sometimes, and another reason she couldn't wait to get out of a business she'd never intended to get involved with. Having grown up on a ranch, she'd handled firearms all her life — but never, ever viewed them as toys.

Schiller's eyes gave off an evil glint. "Well, everyone needs a little fun."

Dex's warnings ghosted through her head. *Guys who enjoy killing. Who love blood.*

A newlywed couple emerged from another lane, beaming in delight. "That was so fun."

For once, Dakota's smile was genuine. "I hope we see you again."

Just not for a divorce party, she hoped.

The happy couple passed her, moving the other way. When Dakota glanced back to make sure Schiller was still with her, she saw one of his men sniff the air as the bride stepped past. The man's eyes closed in rapture, and he licked his lips. Then he traded knowing looks with a second bodyguard counterpart.

Looks that said, *Oh, I bet she would taste good.*

Dakota's skin crawled. It was just as Dex had said. *Like Lucifer reborn. Like creatures of the night.*

Like vampires, the back of her mind filled in.

Which was ridiculous. Still, she wrapped up the tour quickly and headed for the bar.

"Well, those are our main features. Oh, and we recently obtained a liquor license for the bar — strictly limited to after shooting, of course. Can I offer you a drink?"

Schiller's eyes zeroed in on her neck. "Yes, please. I'm parched."

Dakota gritted her teeth. "Wine? Whiskey? Gin?"

Schiller grinned. "Bloody Mary."

She pinned him with her meanest warrior princess stare. As Khloe Maxx, she'd fought two alien invaders and beheaded both — a good vibe to channel right now.

"We don't do mixed drinks."

"What a pity," Schiller said in that creepy monotone.

She shrugged. "I suppose that's something you could institute if you decide to buy in."

All the fucking Bloody Marys you want, she nearly added. *Just not on my watch.*

Her mind spun ahead. If Schiller did buy in, she would have to help Wayne find another job, just in case. Him, she felt duty bound to protect. Darell, on the other hand...

"If we so decide," Schiller murmured, holding her gaze for an eternity.

An eerie, distant chant crept into her ears, and her head went light. All the blood in the back of her body seemed to rush toward the front, making her heart pound.

She clenched her fists. Whoa. Was the man trying to hypnotize her?

She thought of her parents' most vicious dog and her favorite horse, Buck. She thought of her dad, as big and invincible as he'd seemed when she was a kid. Then she pictured native pueblos built high into red rock cliffs. All those strong, impenetrable things. Things that screamed safety, shelter, and *Don't you dare threaten me.*

Finally, Schiller relented, looking slightly miffed.

That's right, asshole, she wanted to say. *No one pushes me around.*

"And what are your plans, Miss Starr?" Schiller asked. "Once you sell your share of the business, I mean? Perhaps you and a business partner plan to..." He scooped the air with a hand.

Her throat was as dry as the Nevada air, but she didn't dare gulp.

She crossed her arms firmly. "I can't see how that's your business."

"Perhaps you intend to open a competing business nearby."

43

She nearly snorted. *Believe me, buddy. Once I get the hell out of Vegas, I'm never coming back.*

But she kept it a businesslike, "I'd be happy to sign a non-compete clause if you like."

He studied her for another too-long minute, then turned to the door. "Thank you for your time, Miss Starr. It's been most informative."

God, she hoped he meant the business, not her.

"I will report to my investors and get back to you soon," Schiller finished. "I promise."

Dakota clenched her jaw. Was that a threat?

"I look forward to it," she lied, holding the door open.

Standing defiantly in that whirling space where the artificially crisp inside air mixed with parched desert heat, she willed them to leave, and leave fast.

"Good night, Miss Starr. It's been a pleasure."

She grimaced, letting the door slam shut. Then she leaned against it and closed her eyes. Holy shit. Wayne hadn't been kidding about *creepy as hell.* And, yeesh. No wonder Dex was so adamant that his bosses were bad to the bone.

She took a deep breath and headed back to the office to tidy up. Well, really, to clear her head. Because, yikes. That had been a lot like the time she'd been set on fire in a special suit. Technically, not all that dangerous, but really intense.

Twenty minutes later, she locked the office and stepped to the exit. Wayne and Darell would shut down the range once their shifts came to an end. Her work was done.

"Bye," she called, though neither could hear her. Then she headed outside and slid into her pickup, more exhausted than she'd been in a long time.

Well, she knew just how to remedy that. A nice, long drive in the desert at night.

Hot Shots was at the edge of the city, so it didn't take long to leave the lights and traffic behind. She rolled down the windows, letting the wind whip her hair while the headlights divided the world into neat slices of night and light.

She let out a long breath. Boy, would it be nice to see Dex.

44

They'd agreed to meet at the Painted Rock parking lot, a twenty-minute drive. One she gradually relaxed into with the help of her favorite Eagles tunes playing from the old-fashioned cassette deck.

Take it easy. . .

But, yikes. There was a storm brewing over the mountains. One of those swirling desert storms full of pent-up electrical energy that flashed and raged.

Still, that would be okay too — to cuddle up with Dex in the pickup while the storm put on a show. Telling him about her meeting with Schiller. Maybe even skipping town. . . fast.

Exiting onto the state park road, she glanced in the rearview mirror. Then she did a double take as three boxy SUVs followed her onto the exit ramp.

Three sets of visitors, at this time of night? All right on her tail?

She twisted to look back, then reached for her phone. But the pickup hit a bump just then, and the phone bounced out of sight.

"Shit."

When the SUVs behind her sped up, she weighed her options. Car chases were not her specialty — not the driving part, at least. And she doubted her pickup could outpace those sleek SUVs.

Still, she floored the gas, desperate for some way out. But there wasn't any, not with lines of boulders hemming in both sides of the road. When one of the SUVs raced up beside her, she slalomed from side to side, denying it space. But the SUV snuck past on a turn and screeched sideways, blocking the road.

Dakota slammed on the brakes. The seat belt caught her with a jerk.

For a moment, the desert was a cacophony of squealing brakes, slamming doors, and shouts. Then everything went eerily still, and a single voice rang out.

"Miss Starr. It seems we have unfinished business."

She stared. Schiller. Igor fucking Schiller, walking toward her like the goddamn King of the Night.

She did her best to turn on the sass. "You have an offer for me?"

Schiller's laugh cracked like shattered glass.

"You might say that."

Chapter Six

Dakota groaned and opened her eyes. At least, she tried to, but they were too heavy. Voices slurred all around her, and the surface under her body was cold and hard.

"New girl, huh?" a man murmured.

"Yeah. Let's see how long she'll last," someone chuckled.

That much, she caught, and both comments made her grimace — echoes of the sexism she'd faced on so many movie sets.

Except, this wasn't a job. This was trouble, sheer trouble. The life-threatening kind.

Her hair lay over one hand, dusty and limp. When she twitched her fingers, her nails dragged along stone, and the scent of urine engulfed her nose. She definitely wasn't in the desert any more. But where was she?

A dungeon was the first thing that came to her groggy mind. A lot like the one she'd escaped in *Knights of Doom*. Mostly, she'd done horse stunts in that movie, but the dungeon scene had also been fun. Which was a hell of a weird thought to entertain at a time like this, but her brain was making the strangest associations right now.

As far as reality went, the last thing she remembered was Schiller's goons closing in on her out in the desert, along with a noxious smell. After that, not much, except the vague sensation of being carried, dumped in a back seat, and driven somewhere. Where, she had no idea, because she'd faded out along the way.

Now, metal ground against metal — a key turning in a lock? — and booted feet clomped off into the distance, leaving her in a muted void.

A void she floated in for — minutes? hours? — before trying to open her eyes again. Finally, she succeeded, though her surroundings were cloaked in shadows. In the distance, yellowish light filtered in, and she rolled toward it, stifling another groan. God, did her head spin.

"You okay, lady?" a softer, kinder voice whispered.

Slowly, she worked her hands and knees under her body and wobbled to all fours, muttering, "Great."

The man, whoever he was, chuckled.

She blinked and looked around. Dungeon was an apt term. Or rather, a dungeon crossed with a Western jail — the kind with a long row of barred cells. A second row of cells faced hers, with a long walkway separating both sides. The only light came from either end of the walkway, with voices in the distance. Guards?

Slowly, she rose to unsteady feet, gripping the cell's bars for support.

"Good way to lose a hand, honey," her neighbor warned, tapping it.

When she snapped back her hand, he laughed.

"Oh, I won't hurt you. But Fang over there will." He nodded to the cell on her opposite side.

A snarl rose from the darkness. Something big and furry moved, and long, ivory teeth flashed in the dim light.

Dakota stared. Was that a bear? An oversized boar?

"Back off," she snapped in a no-nonsense tone that worked on ferocious dogs.

The snarl broke off abruptly, followed by a confused whine. Then the beast — whatever it was — sighed, flopped back on its haunches, and scratched an ear with its back paw.

Dakota turned away slowly, keeping her arms out for balance. Her senses were gradually coming back into focus, though it was hard to see in the dark. Somewhere to the left, muffled cheers sounded, along with the clang of steel against steel.

"What is this place?"

"The Pits, honey," said the man in the adjoining cell. "We're five stories below the Scarlet Palace."

"The Pits?"

"A fighting arena, like the Colosseum. Don't you know? It's run by Schiller and his bloodsucking goons."

The man's words rang a bell, and Dakota peered over, slowly adjusting to the dim light. He was tall, lean, and pale, just like Schiller and his goons. Unlike them, he was clad entirely in white, though the fabric was smeared with dirt.

"Wait. You're the guy from that protest group, aren't you?"

The man grinned and bent into an exaggerated bow. "Alon Edgar, at your service."

She hesitated, then replied. "Dakota Starr."

His eyes went wide. "Dakota Starr? *The* Dakota Starr?"

Dakota nearly groaned. The average moviegoer had no idea who she was, but aficionados like Wayne — and apparently this guy, Alon — seemed to keep tabs on the who's who of the stunt world.

"Oh my God. I'm such a fan. I love all your work, but the warrior princess Khloe Maxx..." He slashed an imaginary sword. "Stand back, asshole!"

"Yeah, well... Thanks."

She hid a sigh, then tested the bars with a hard shake. They didn't budge, which might have been a good thing, considering the hairy beast lurking to her left.

"What's up with this place? And don't the police know?"

"The police don't want to know, honey. And if they did, they would run screaming, like most humans do."

"Humans? As opposed to...?"

Alon shrugged. "Vampires, of course." When he caught her look, he flapped a hand. "I know, I know, you don't believe me. And out in the human world, that wouldn't matter. But if you want to survive down here, you ought to know. No, you *need* to know."

She turned away, focusing on the light at the end of the walkway. Clearly, Alon had lost his mind. And she had no time to waste. Somehow, she had to escape.

"Look, honey," Alon hissed. "Just look."

She peered down the hallway. "Not now."

49

"Look at me," he insisted. But that time, the word slurred, because something was wrong with his mouth.

Dakota froze as his canines extended into fangs and his eyes took on a red glow.

"What the...?"

"See?" Alon lisped, tipping his head left and right so she could get a good look. "God, it's so hard to talk with these things," he muttered as the fangs retracted again.

Dakota stood still. That was some kind of trick, right?

Then she remembered the rally that had helped her escape the Scarlet Palace unnoticed the day she'd found Dex. All those picketers chanting, *Stop the bloodsuckers!*

She froze. Literally?

"Don't worry." Alon blinked the red glow from his eyes. "Unlike the unenlightened heathens who run this place, I don't drink blood."

Still not sure she believed him, Dakota kept him talking. "You don't?"

"Of course not. Who knows what's in human blood?"

Dakota thought that one over. Maybe he had a point.

"I've been vegan for three years now, and I've never felt better. Look at me!" Alon turned from side to side as if to show off a wonderful new figure. "I feel better. I look better. I have more energy. And best of all, I sleep soundly at night."

Dakota blinked. A vegan vampire?

"What do you drink, then?"

"Oh, you know... Gazpacho, beet juice, tomato juice... and soy-based substitutes, of course. It's amazing what you can do with soy these days. In fact, there's a great place just off Fremont Street..." he gushed, then trailed off with a sigh. "I swear, if I make it out of here alive, that's the first place I'll go."

Dakota made a face. Her first step would be getting the hell out of Dodge. Vampires or not, she'd had enough of Vegas.

Then her stomach sank. What about Dex? Where was he? Was he all right?

The creature in the next cell shook its pelt and began pacing, as did several of the other prisoners. Some were human and some were animals, while others...

She stared at the inmate in the cell opposite hers. Wait. Hadn't that been a man? Now, all she saw was a wolf. It sat on its haunches and raised its muzzle in a plaintive howl.

Someone threw a steel dish. "Shut up, John."

Dakota furrowed her brow. A wolf named John?

"Shifter," Alon explained with another sad sigh. "Now that you're here, you might as well know."

"Shifter." Her voice was perfectly even, unlike her nerves.

Alon nodded. "You know, like a werewolf." Then he brightened. "Did you ever do a movie with werewolves?"

She shook her head.

"Too bad." Alon frowned. "Then again, Hollywood usually gets them wrong. I have to say, *Spartacus Revamped* was full of stereotypes. I mean, seriously — the capes were all wrong, even for a period piece." Then he stuck up his hands. "I still loved your part, though. Cosima Canddell sure knows how to kick ass."

Dakota rolled her eyes and muttered her usual line. "I just did the stunts."

"They were the best part, honey."

Dakota sighed. That was true of most of the movies she'd been in.

Alon went on and on about vampires and shifters for a while, describing an entire parallel world most humans were unaware of. Apparently, most species kept to themselves, but some intermixed.

"My cousin Melody eloped with a dragon shifter. Her parents still insist it was a huge mistake, but I say they need to get with the times..."

Alon droned on about vampires, werebears, then gargoyles. Gargoyles! He was just segueing into some nonsense about a pack of wolves who ran a nearby casino when the light at the end of the walkway flickered.

Dakota pressed against the front of the cell, trying to make out who — or what — that was.

"This way," one of two figures silhouetted by the light whispered.

All around Dakota, caged men and beasts rose to their feet, and a cloud of agitation crept over the place. Some growled while others muttered aloud.

"Shh. Don't raise the guards."

Which suggested the two men striding down the walkway weren't guards. Their furtive looks reinforced the impression, as did their quick, quiet steps.

"Dakota?" one whisper-hissed.

Every nerve in her body tensed, then warmed.

"Dex? Dex!" she cried when he drew into the light.

He grabbed her hands through the bars of the cell and pressed in close. "Are you all right? Please tell me you're all right."

The creature to Dakota's left snarled and pawed at the bars, but one harsh, commanding growl from Dex made the beast retreat to the back of his cell.

"I'm okay. I have no idea what's going on, but I'm okay." Then she clenched a fist. "I could kill Schiller, though."

Dex snorted. "Me first." He kissed her hands and cupped her cheek. Then he turned to the smaller man beside him. "Hurry up, Bob. Get her out."

Bob fumbled with a ring of keys bigger than a frisbee. The keys jangled and clanged against the cell bars, making Dex wince. "Quiet!"

The prisoners grew increasingly agitated, and one of them hissed, "Watch out!"

The doors at one end of the hall slammed open, flooding the walkway with light.

"Shit." Dex spun and raised his fists, ready for a fight.

Bob squeaked, dropped the keys, and shrank back. Literally. He hunched and grew smaller and smaller until only a pile of clothes remained. Then a small, bristly animal emerged from the heap — a hedgehog scurrying to safety through the shadows.

"See?" Alon said, not too helpfully. "Shifter."

Dakota had no idea what had just happened, but she knew trouble when she saw it. She tapped Dex. "Go. Get out of here."

"No way. I got you into this. I'll get you out."

Four big, burly guards rushed at him, and she cried, "You have to go!"

But he didn't budge. All he did was look over with those dark, soulful eyes. "I love you, Dakota. Whatever happens next, remember that. Please."

His voice held a scary, *As a gentleman, I must go down with the* Titanic tone, and she rattled the bars. "No, Dex. Go. Please."

But he didn't go. He bared his teeth at the approaching guards and let loose a terrifying growl. A real growl.

"Dex..." Dakota whispered desperately.

Then her jaw fell open, because Dex's body began to transform. His back curved, and his nails grew to claws. His shirt split down the back, and—

Dakota stared as her lover's ebony skin disappeared beneath jet-black fur.

Alon whistled. "Black panther. Haven't seen one of those for a while."

Dakota gaped. Panther?

She jumped back as the feline and the guards erupted into a vicious fight, eliciting cheers from the prisoners. Most seemed to be on Dex's side, but their bloodthirsty cries made Dakota sick.

"Just wait till you see the Pits," Alon murmured, reading her mind.

Dakota would rather not. But would she have a choice?

More guards rushed in. Some human, armed with pikes or nets, others beasts, including wolves and bears. As fiercely as Dex fought, he was badly outnumbered, and—

"Get the door!" someone yelled.

One of the guards grabbed the fallen key ring and opened the door to Dakota's cell. If she'd had her wits about her, she might have used the chance to slip out, but all she could do was stare. The gang of guards forced the hissing, slashing panther

53

to back into her cell. Then they slammed the door shut and turned the key.

The panther lashed out between the bars, while the guards jumped back, panting.

"Shit, man. Can't wait to see him in the ring," someone muttered.

Another of the guards clenched his bleeding shoulder. "He'll be the main event, I bet. But, fuck. I pity the fool who has to report this to Schiller."

Muttering and stumbling, the guards retreated. When the doors slammed behind them, cutting off most of the light, a wary silence fell over the prison.

When the panther had been forced into her cell, Dakota had flattened herself against the rear wall. Now, as he paced, she leaned forward.

"Dex?" Her wavering voice drifted through the near-silent ward.

When the panther turned, the dark eyes meeting hers were familiar. Intimately so.

She crouched, extending a shaky hand. "Dex, is it really you?"

Chapter Seven

Dex took one careful step toward Dakota, then another. God, this was it. The make-or-break moment when she would accept or reject his shifter side. He crouched, making himself as small as possible. But his tail kept whipping hopefully, and his whiskers twitched.

Cut that out, he ordered his feline side.

Shh, his panther breathed dreamily as Dakota reached out.

The moment she touched his head, his heart thumped harder. And when she started gently scratching his ears...

That feels so good. His panther closed its eyes to savor her scent.

Yes, it did. So good, he nearly forgot where he was and why.

But then she whispered his name, and it all came back in a rush.

Dungeon. Cell. Deep underground.

He swung his head from side to side, using his keen shifter senses to study his surroundings. The cell on the left had the dank, musty smell of boar — a huge, wild one, more beast than human. The guy on the right emitted no scent at all. Dex bared his teeth and growled. Vampire. Too bad it wasn't Schiller, locked up as he deserved to be.

Somewhere farther down the row of cells was an angry bear, a couple of bitter wolves, and at least one rhino shifter. Some were in animal form, others human, like the beady-eyed aardvark shifter across the way. There was no hint of Bob, who'd slunk off just in time. At least there was that — hope of help from the outside.

But, shoot. *Outside* meant beyond the prison block within the complex deep below the Scarlet Palace. How had it ever come to this?

He gave his tail one last, angry swipe and shifted, coming slowly to his feet.

"Dakota," he whispered, voice scratchy with the last traces of his feline side.

Her eyes were wide and her voice was a little shaky, but she crossed her arms with her usual sass.

"Boy, do you have a lot of explaining to do."

He bobbed his head. Yes, he did.

She frowned. "Wait. How the hell does that work? Do it again."

If she'd been any other soul on the planet, he would have refused. He wasn't a circus pony trained to do tricks.

You got a problem with circus ponies? a deep voice growled in his mind — the Clydesdale shifter from a few cells down.

Ignoring him, Dex flexed his fingers and released his panther again. Slowly, painfully, so Dakota could see it wasn't a trick. Just him, shifting from one body to another. Back in panther form, he strutted around in a circle, letting her look.

The Clydesdale snorted. *Now who's the circus pony, asshole?*

Dex nearly hissed back, but that might alarm Dakota. Besides, there was a certain satisfaction to revealing his second side to his mate.

I think she likes me, his panther hummed.

Man, he sure hoped so. Slowly, he shifted back and stood on two feet.

Dakota blinked a few times. "How does that work?"

He shrugged. "Never really thought about it. It just does."

For a moment there, she'd softened with wonder, but now, she went back to crossing her arms.

"And you were going to tell me — when?"

Um, never? Soon? Frankly, he had no idea what to say, because he was improvising, as usual.

"I wanted to tell you, but I never got the chance."

56

Dakota shook her head furiously. "Dammit, Dex. We've been sleeping together for six weeks, and you never found a chance?"

Every head in the long row of cells turned.

"Seriously, man? Six weeks?" the vampire in the next cell scolded.

"What were you thinking?" the bear a little farther down added.

He was thinking... um... uh...

He showed his teeth and thundered into their minds. *Shut up!*

The cellblock fell silent, while Dakota went red. Her brow furrowed when she glanced up and down the row of cells. "Wait. Were you... talking to them?"

He winced. "Not exactly."

She stuck her hand on her hip. God, was she gorgeous when she was mad.

"Not exactly?"

Damn. This was going downhill, fast. "We can communicate through our thoughts."

She looked around, definitely not amused. "So, you'll talk to these bozos but you never talked to me? Really talked, I mean."

"Not a way to win over your girl," the vampire tut-tutted.

That time, both Dex and Dakota turned to yell, "Shut up!"

Then she turned back, redder than ever. "Any other secrets you were planning to keep?"

"None! I mean..."

Her chin snapped up, and her nostrils flared. "Yes?"

Wow. Dakota truly was something when she was riled up. Like she was in bed after shedding that outer layer of self-control.

She tapped her foot impatiently and barked, "Come on, already. And no bullshit. No secrets."

The hay on the floor of the other cells rustled as everyone leaned closer.

Then she stuck up her hands and winced. "No, wait. Put something on, for goodness' sake."

Oops. He'd forgotten that his clothes had shredded in his shift. Luckily, a fellow prisoner took mercy and tossed a pair of sweat pants through the bars of the cell.

"Thanks," Dex muttered, yanking them on.

His panther side mourned. Dakota had seen him naked plenty of times, and vice versa. But those tender, private moments seemed so far away now.

He stepped closer, dropping his voice. "Okay, no secrets." His mind spun, wondering where to start. "Um... My name's not really Dex."

Her eyes flashed. "No? What, then? George? Henry? Roger?"

"Roger?" he protested.

She made a stirring motion, prompting him.

He glanced around, then whispered.

Dakota tilted her head. "What?"

He huffed and looked around. No one beyond his family knew his real name. No one.

"What are you all looking at?" he muttered.

Everyone whipped away — except the aardvark. Dex flung a pebble at the jerk then leaned closer to Dakota, whispering so only she could hear.

Or maybe she couldn't, because she cupped a hand to her ear. "What was that?" Then she threw up her hands. "Dammit, Dex, is this how you communicate?"

He gritted his teeth and bellowed, "It's Poindexter, okay?"

The vampire behind her smirked, and someone chuckled in the darkness beyond. Shoot. Even if he survived the Pits, he was never going to live this down.

"Oh. Okay, what else?" she demanded as if that wasn't enough. Didn't she know how personal that was to him?

No, his panther pointed out. *She doesn't because you never talk to her.*

He pursed his lips. His two biggest secrets in one day, and she wanted more?

Then it hit him what other secret he had — one he really ought to tell her now that he was baring all. But, damn. Being destined mates was the hardest to explain of all.

"There's one more," he whispered, half hoping she wouldn't hear.

She studied him wearily. "You're gay?"

All up and down the cellblock, ears perked.

"No!"

The corners of her mouth hinted at a teasing grin. "Okay, Mr. Touchy. What is it, then?"

You're my mate. He turned the words over in his mind, wondering what she might say.

"Not sure you want to know," he finally admitted.

She sighed, leaning against the stone wall. "You're right. I'm not sure I do."

For a moment, silence reigned. Then Dakota turned to the aardvark. "Do you think I want to know?"

The aardvark looked between Dex and her, then shrugged. "Hard to tell. Ignorance is bliss, but knowledge is power."

Dex threw another pebble at him. "You're not supposed to be listening, man."

The aardvark scuttled to the farthest possible corner of his cell. A tension-packed silence filled the massive hall while Dakota pondered his advice.

"Okay, tell me," she finally whispered.

"Are you sure?"

She ground her teeth. "No, I'm not. But tell me anyway."

He took a deep breath. "You're my... my... "

She scooped the air with her hand, drawing it out of him. "My... "

Just then, the doors at the end of the hallway banged open again, and several tall figures strode down the hall.

Dex stepped forward. If those thugs planned to separate him from Dakota, they had another thing coming.

But it wasn't just thugs making everyone withdraw to the shadows of their cells. The big boss himself was there.

"Well, well." Igor Schiller's eyes bored into Dex, then Dakota. "Mr. Davitt and Miss Starr, happily reunited here in the Scarlet Palace."

"More like the bowels of the Scarlet Palace," Dakota muttered, emphasizing *bowels.*

"A pity you're not satisfied with your accommodations. But I'm afraid this is what happens when one arrives unannounced." Schiller's eyes glowed red.

Dex resisted glaring back. Defying Schiller meant gambling not only with his life, but with Dakota's. So, he threw out the only ace he had in a desperate hope of a deal.

"Let Dakota go, and I'll return the money."

"Ah, yes," Schiller sighed. "The stolen money."

"Not stolen. We played by the rules."

Schiller snorted. "Perhaps you played by the rules of blackjack. However, as an employee..." His tone dropped to a threat.

Dex gripped the bars of the cell, hinting at how hard he would squeeze Schiller's neck when he got the chance.

"Do you want to know where the money is or not? Without me, you'll never find it."

Schiller shrugged. "We have a great deal of money. What you stole is our pride."

"Pride?" The vampire in the neighboring cell piped up. "How can you speak of pride, you bloodsucking maggot? You're a disgrace to all vampires. Don't you know times have changed?"

Schiller turned slowly toward him. "You, Alon, are the disgrace. But worry not. I have plans for you."

Then he turned to study Dex and Dakota. So quietly and for so long, Dex's skin crawled. What did the vampire have in mind?

Something gruesome, judging by the way Schiller slowly licked his lips. "Luckily, Mr. Davitt and Miss Starr have chosen to visit at a most opportune time. I happen to be expecting some important guests, for whom I shall be throwing a feast." He leaned closer, grinning. "A very special kind of feast."

Dex's stomach turned. He'd heard of the "feasts" Schiller threw for VIPs — multi-course events featuring delicacies that vampires sampled like so many fine wines. The blood of a virgin, delivered fresh from the vein. Entire smorgasbords of exotic animal flavors, from giraffe to gazelle. The main course would be devoted to fresh shifter blood, culminating in the rarest of the rare for dessert — drops of imported unicorn or dragon blood rumored to have cost hundreds of thousands of dollars.

Some of the blood "donors" survived, and some didn't. The stories were so gory and so outrageous, Dex had never really believed them. But now, he wasn't so sure.

Alon snorted loudly. "What a waste."

Schiller flicked a hand, unimpressed. "You are hardly qualified to judge."

"I may not be, but I know a missed business opportunity when I see one." Alon turned his back abruptly.

Schiller frowned, and his eyes narrowed while Alon muttered away. "Go ahead. Miss your chance to revive flagging interest in the Pits..."

Schiller's eyes darkened as he turned to one of his men. One Dex recognized as Bernie, entertainment manager for the Scarlet Palace. When Schiller raised one eyebrow sharply, the man dragged a foot nervously through the dirt.

"We're experiencing a temporary dip in revenue. All perfectly normal, sir."

Alon snorted. "Every supernatural in town knows the Lone Wolf Casino is where the action is these days, what with their new mermaid show."

Schiller flapped a hand. "Fake mermaids. Any vampire can tell from one sniff. How anyone falls for that, I don't know."

"The point is, they do," Alon noted.

Schiller considered, then shot Bernie an icy look.

"Not to worry, sir," the manager hurried to add. "We have a thrilling new show planned."

Schiller's features grew even tighter. "How thrilling?"

Alon yawned. "Let me guess. More gladiator fights. So passé."

Bernie shook his head quickly. "Something even bigger. Better. Newer..."

Schiller stirred the air with his hand.

Bernie gulped, leaned in, and whispered. Dex couldn't catch a word, except for Bernie's final promise. "Death around every corner."

Schiller broke into a satisfied smile. "There, you see?"

Dex gritted his teeth. No, he didn't.

Alon didn't look impressed. "And who is going to last long enough to guarantee a good show?" He gestured toward the other cells. "That slow-witted rhino? That aging boar?"

The boar growled, while the rhino shifter growled, "Slow-witted? Says who?"

"You need close calls," Alon said. "Hair-raising escapes! Dripping blood! And these two, I believe, are just what you need." He pointed to Dex and Dakota.

Dex shot him a killer look. *Speak for yourself, asshole.*

But Schiller tapped his pale lips, studying the two of them in a whole new way.

"I must admit, it has potential," Schiller murmured.

Dex ground his teeth. Potential to kill his true love — and him?

Schiller frowned. "However, there is the matter of my feast..."

"This is far better than a feast," Alon cut in. "And what a message it would send! The panther who thought he could scam you out of a million dollars paying the ultimate price."

Dex kicked at the cell bars. "Not helping, asshole."

Then he did a double take, because Alon winked. A *trust me* wink that hinted at some master plan.

Dex frowned. A vampire's master plan wasn't something to bank your life on.

Schiller stroked his chin slowly. "I suppose it has some merit."

"Merit?" Alon snorted. "Feasts are all well and good, but a good fight will rake in millions. Millions. Tell him, Bernie."

"Millions, sir," Bernie agreed. "Especially if you consider tickets, concessions, merchandising..."

Dakota shot Dex a look and mouthed, *Merchandising?*

Dex frowned. Did that mean action figures of him and Dakota that could be dismembered then reassembled for hours of bloodthirsty fun?

Alon nodded enthusiastically. "Good plan."

Bernie beamed.

"Of course, if you want a really good show, you would treat your fighters well." Alon shuffled through the hay at his feet in disdain. "How you expect anyone to perform well after enduring such conditions, I don't know."

"It's perfectly adequate," Schiller sniffed.

Alon snorted. "So is running second to the Lone Wolf Casino."

Schiller's hands formed fists, and his pale cheeks showed a flash of color. "We will never run second to those accursed wolves!" Then he turned his burning red eyes on Bernie.

His entertainment manager jumped back. "Sir?"

Schiller raised one eyebrow, maintaining a chilling silence.

Bernie gulped. "Well, our last star lasted months when we granted him a few perks."

Schiller scowled. "Perks?"

Bernie nodded. "Premium suite cell, meals from upstairs..."

Alon nodded along. "Kyrill headlined your fights for weeks, correct?" Then he sighed. "Oh, those were the days. It's been all downhill since then."

Dex made a face. Kyrill probably would have agreed, especially the day he'd finally met an untimely death in the Pits.

But Alon kept up that look that said, *Roll with this, buddy. I swear, it will work.*

Schiller considered for another minute, then snapped his fingers. "Guards, transfer these two to the premium suite cell." Then he flashed a cruel smile. "Enjoy your new accommodations, Mr. Davitt, Miss Starr. Or should I say, enjoy them while you can."

With that, he about-faced and strode for the exit. Minutes later, Dex and Dakota were forced out of their cell and marched down the central walkway. Dozens of eyes followed them, some jealous, others full of pity.

"You're loco, man," one of the guards muttered at Dex. "Why didn't you just take the money and run?"

The obvious answer was *I wish I had.* But, no. That wasn't true.

He looked over at Dakota, striding at his side, then murmured without breaking eye contact, "Because I love her. Simple as that. I will love her to the end of my days."

Chapter Eight

When the door slammed behind Dakota, she gulped. Not so much at the sound of a heavy lock turning, but from what Dex had said.

I will love her to the end of my days.

Her lips wobbled, and she stared at Dex. Everything had happened so quickly, she'd had no time to think things through. But now that she mulled it over...

That guard was right. Dex could have left Vegas with the money weeks ago. And, hell. He hadn't had to risk everything to try to free her now.

She gulped. "That's true. You could have left and avoided this mess."

His throat bobbed, and a moment later, he shook his head. "Not going anywhere without you."

She crossed her arms. "I'm still mad, you know." It was a matter of principle.

Dex laughed. "That's one of the things I love about you." Then his face fell. "But I never expected it to come to this. I never wanted you in danger."

Her heart thumped a little faster, a little harder. "Love, huh?"

He nodded. "Love. For real. Forever." He flashed a weak smile. "I'm sorry it took me so long to figure it out. I guess I'm quicker with cards than with love."

Her emotions swirled, because part of her still wanted to be mad. But another part wanted to grab on to that *forever* part and never let go.

One moment later, her defenses crumbled, and she threw her arms around him. Then she snuggled in for the world's tightest, *never letting go* hug.

"Maybe we were both slow to figure it out," she murmured into his neck. Dex had a way of driving her crazy at times — but she'd never had as much fun with anyone as with him, and she'd ever felt so alive. And, heck — it was like that guard said. Dex could have taken the money and run.

She held him tightly, then drew back just far enough for a kiss. A short, serious one that said, *I love you, but whoa, are we in deep shit.*

Dex nuzzled her cheek with the perfect line of his beard, a sensation she loved — half stubbly, half smooth. Then he sighed and looked around. "You're right. We are in some deep shit."

She did a double take. Had he just read her mind? Then it hit her — was that a shifter thing, the way he'd communicated with the others in their cells?

Well, if it was, she wasn't ready to get into those details quite yet. Instead, she waved a hand, feigning a lighter tone. "Well, we did get upgraded to the VIP cell."

"Kind of an oxymoron, don't you think?"

She sighed. "Definitely. But maybe there's a better chance of breaking out of here."

She started pacing around. Dex did the same, and together, they inspected every inch of the place. No windows or air ducts to escape through, as she'd done on the set of *Deal of Death*. No access to electronics to set off false alarms. As far as security went, the place was as tight as Alcatraz.

As far as creature comforts, on the other hand...

A flat-screen TV took up most of one wall, and the mini-bar was stocked with snacks and drinks. One door led to a bathroom bigger than her apartment, with big, fluffy towels, a shower and separate bathtub, plus a steaming Jacuzzi. A side door brought her to a walk-in closet packed with clothes in every conceivable size, and another revealed a sauna. Yet another door opened onto a private training gym half the size of a basketball court, with weights and weapons locked in a sturdy display case.

She sighed and went back to the living room, thumping the Scarlet Palace stationery on the desk.

"Does Schiller think I'm going to write a will and leave everything to him?"

Dex didn't answer. He was too engrossed in the gold-framed portraits on the walls, each showing a ferocious man or animal.

She stepped over. "Let me guess. The fighting pit hall of fame?"

Dex nodded slowly. "Something like that."

She squinted at the labels, then paled. The one named Kyrill seemed to hold the dubious record — twelve weeks before meeting his untimely demise.

She stepped over to the king-size bed and flopped back, staring at the ceiling.

Well, she intended to, but it was a water bed, and the whole thing started rolling and heaving like the North Atlantic in a gale. When it finally settled down, she whispered, "Maybe you should have grabbed the money and run."

Dex came over to join her, setting off another tsunami. He cursed, and when the wave action finally subsided, he whispered, "No regrets."

God, she loved that bass of his.

"Not even in getting involved in the first place?"

He mulled it over, then shook his head. "Not even that. Tanner's cause was a good one — blocking a casino in a pristine place. And my sister could have done amazing things with my share of the winnings."

Dakota's throat went dry at his use of the past tense. Still, she coaxed him on, eager to learn more. "Your sister?"

Dex laid it all out for her, explaining the details of the *Save the Florida Panther* foundation and how closely that paralleled Tanner's mission to protect the forest treasured by his bear clan.

When she thought it over, what they'd done was a lot more *Robin Hood* than *heist*.

"For the first time in my life, I had a mission, too — a good one. . . " Her heart swelled at the hope and pride in Dex's voice, then sank at his mournful sigh. "I just wish we could do something to shut down Schiller for good."

She jutted her chin from side to side, thinking it through. "Let's start with getting out of here alive." Carefully, she rolled to face him and stroked the neat outlines of his boxy beard. "Okay, think positive. Let's say we win this fight they have planned."

"Even if we did, it's not much help. The more you win in the Pits, the more they throw at you in the next fight." Dex shook his head. "Besides, these are shifters and vampires. What are you going to do against them? They don't exactly provide weapons in there. Not weapons you know about anyway."

"Try me," she growled.

"I've only ever seen one fight. One guy had this weird, curvy sword. . . "

He shaped something with his hands, and even that small motion set off a ripple in the bed.

"You mean a *sica?*"

He stared. "A what?"

She rolled her eyes. "*Spartacus Revamped* had a historical consultant on the set. I had to wrestle a tiger, then grab the Thraex's sword, and then finish off the Retiarius. You know — the guy with the trident."

He blinked. "Trident?"

She tapped his chest. "Maybe you're the one we need to worry about, champ. Especially if a Retiarius comes at you with a net."

His expression went totally blank, which made her worry more. Then he flapped his hands. "Whatever. It's not rehearsed like a movie, Dakota. And they sure as hell don't worry about injuries or insurance down here."

Despair gnawed at the edges of her soul. "Are you saying there's no hope?"

"I'm saying our chances are slim."

She stared at the ceiling a little longer, then sighed. "Any idea how long we have until they come for us?"

Dex's face went grim. "Friday night fights bring in the biggest crowds. That gives us forty-eight hours, give or take."

A lump formed in her throat. Forty-eight hours left to live?

She did her best not to let it show. "So, we need a plan. Fast."

Dex looked over at her. "I hate to say it, but plans have a way of falling apart." Then he brightened. "On the other hand, I never planned on meeting you, and that was a good thing."

She chuckled, then grew serious. "That's the trick, I guess — to come prepared with a plan, but be prepared to improvise too."

Dex grinned. "That, I can do."

She thought it over. The best stunt teams made the most of everyone's strengths. So that was as good a place as any to begin. She could make the plan — and several backups — while trusting Dex to improvise when the time came.

Which brought her to the second key element of a team. Trust.

She locked eyes with Dex, then surprised herself with a firm nod. She could trust him.

"I trust you too," Dex whispered, squeezing her hand.

She stared at the ceiling a little longer, then prepared to get to her feet. But between the awkward motion of the water bed and Dex taking her hand, she didn't get far.

"There's one more thing I need to tell you." His voice had a scary note of resignation, like a man headed to the gallows.

"Fine." She settled back again, faking a sigh. But in truth, her ears had perked at his words. "Something other than you can change into a panther, you're not gay, and your real name is Poindexter?"

For a long time, he just looked at her. Then he whispered, "You're my destined mate."

Dakota's mind blanked. "Destined what?"

He pursed his lips, searching for words. "My mate. My destiny." Then he shook his head and muttered, "It's a shifter thing."

Like so many times before, they lay on a bed, side-by-side and face-to-face. And yet, it was totally different, because they weren't playing around any more. His eyes were so dark and so sincere. His voice was full of yearning. A different side of Dex — one he didn't reveal often.

He touched her shoulder. "Shifters have more senses than humans do. Not just a sense of smell, space, sight, touch, or taste. A sense of... Well, destiny. Telling us when we've found the one."

The way he said it gave her the impression of words so important, they were capitalized. *The One.*

"The one you're meant to be with forever. The one you will always love."

She stared. His eyes shone with hope — and fear. Fear of what — that she would reject him? Even now that she knew what he'd done for her?

"Humans call it soul mates, but they're not very good at recognizing the real deal," he went on. "But shifters are. Because when you meet her — the person fate sent you, because you belong together forever — you know." Then he frowned. "Well, shifters are supposed to be able to tell. It took me a while to catch on, but now I know. And fate doesn't make mistakes the way people do. When you find your mate, that's it. You cherish her. Love her. Protect her to the end of your days."

Her heart swelled, then ached, because what if that end was nearer than either of them wanted to admit?

"I see," she said slowly. "And that's that? You just know, and it's a done deal?"

Dex nodded earnestly. "When you know, you know."

She swallowed, remembering the way time had screeched to a stop the day they'd met... The way her body and soul seemed to rejoice every time she woke in Dex's arms... All those times she'd bumped into furniture or stammered over simple words...

She reached out and rested a hand on his shoulder, wondering about destiny.

Then she took a deep breath. "Forever, huh?"

He nodded. "Forever. If you can live with a guy like me."

She bit her lip. Dex did have some infuriating faults. But, hell — she did too. And wasn't the rest more important? The way he could make her feel like a queen with one yearning look. The way he made her laugh, and the way he made her dream.

She did her best to look stern but failed miserably. "I don't think I can live without you. Same thing?"

With a laugh, he pulled her into a hug, setting the bed into another series of waves. "Good enough for me."

She closed her eyes, the better to soak it all in. The scratch in his voice. The *I'll never let you down* determination in his firm touch. The *Please don't say no* tilt to his shoulders, and the inner tension that promised, *But if you do say no, I will respect that and let you go. It may kill me, but I will let you go.*

That was what she loved about him. The way he respected her word. And, hell — a guy who could bring her hope in a situation as dire as this had to be the real thing.

She hung on to him for a long time, mind swirling with deep thoughts she hadn't let herself entertain before. Thoughts of love, forever, and fate. But, yikes. Given their current predicament...

As always, Dex seemed to read her mind.

"Lots to process, I know. But first things first. We need a plan. And knowing how well my plans turn out..." He sighed. "Any great ideas, boss?"

Chapter Nine

A few minutes wasn't enough to plan what might be the last forty-eight hours of her life, but Dakota did her best.

The thing was, she was so tired, she couldn't think straight. No matter how hard she tried, the jumble of worries in her mind tangled into ever-tighter knots.

But with Dex wrapping his arms around her — keeping very still so as not to set off more waves in the stupid water bed — that jumble faded away, leaving her with a sense of peace. Within minutes, she nodded off.

And, yikes. She didn't just nod off. She slept like a log, as she discovered upon opening her eyes and checking the clock. Five hours had slipped by in the blink of an eye and left her refreshed.

Dex woke at about the same time and brushed her hair back from her face. "You okay?"

"Pretty good. You?"

He flashed her a bolstering smile. "Surprisingly good. So good, I'd be tempted to stay here a little longer, if you know what I mean."

When he tickled her ribs, she grinned. Oh, she knew what he meant, all right. A little more touching and a few not-so-innocent kisses were all it would take to put them in an entirely different mood. A sensual one, in which they left their worries behind while indulging in the kind of soul-satisfying sex that was always guaranteed with Dex.

"I'm tempted, too," she admitted. "But training comes first."

When he groaned, she laughed. "Think of it this way. Training could help us survive, and then we'll have all the time we want." She leaned over, kissing his perfect lips.

"Mm. Promise?"

She would have laughed, but the enormity of it hit her. She couldn't promise, because too much was out of her control.

"I promise to do my best."

Dex nodded solemnly, and they both rolled out of bed. Minutes later, after they'd both downed some cereal with milk from the minibar, then headed to the training gym.

"Aha," A few minutes into rooting around the place, she found a short, curved sword. "It's rubber, but it will work for practice."

When she tossed it to Dex, he caught it and gave it a few swipes. "A *sica*, right?"

She grinned. The man really had been listening.

He was a quick study too. Soon, they were slicing, thrusting, and chopping at thin air, then at each other.

"Too bad there's only one sword," she lamented.

Dex grinned and tossed it back to her. "No problem. I have a different weapon."

She tilted her head, wondering what he had found. But when he stripped off his shirt and pants—

"Oh." She stepped back with a gulp. "That."

That was the ripple of muscles giving way to an entirely new shape. A short, sleek covering of fur. Fingernails that elongated and curved into claws. A long, graceful tail that swished this way and that.

Dakota forced herself to take several deep breaths. Right — Dex's shifter side.

A minute or two of gazing into those deep, dark eyes kept her calm, though, and soon, they eased into a style of sparring she had never imagined. Dex came at her carefully at first, raising a paw in a slow-motion swipe. She met it with a soft tap of her sword, then forced the lump in her throat away.

"Okay. Let's try it again, but faster."

In no time, they were in the throes of a mock battle, whirling into and out of attacks. The terror of facing down a wild beast slowly faded, and she learned not to overextend, aim too high, or underestimate the stability four feet lent her opponent. It took all her concentration — and strength — to repel Dex's lightning-fast attacks, but she did it. When he stepped up the pace and came at her with even more ferocious strikes, she managed to dodge, retreat, or even launch a counterattack.

As challenging as it was, it was also fun. At least, as long as she didn't think about why they were practicing in the first place.

By then, she was sweating up a storm, but Dex's fur was smooth and velvety — so much so, she had to remind herself not to touch just for the joy of it. His eyes danced as he fought intently — not so much concentrating on his own defense as making sure he kept his claws tucked safely away. When they broke apart, panting after every round of sparring, his tail lashed proudly as if to say, *I'm impressed.*

Impressed with my mate, his voice ghosted faintly through her mind. Or was she imagining things?

Then he yowled and launched himself at her in a huge leap. Dakota shoved and sliced, but a moment later, he pounced, pinning her to the ground.

Gotcha, his shining eyes said.

The view up into that ferocious feline face was more thrilling than terrifying, and Dakota couldn't help running her hands up his smooth, bulky shoulders. His eyes sparkled, so she reached a little farther and rubbed around his silky, triangular ears.

The panther — Dex — tilted his head, closed his eyes, and... purred?

She closed her eyes, soaking in the sensation. She was the one pinned to the ground, yet all she sensed was power and a warm, pulsing sensation in her soul.

When the panther gently nuzzled her cheek, she squeaked, then chuckled, thinking back to all the times Dex had done that when they were in bed. At the time, she'd had no idea he was a shifter, but now, it all fit.

The longer they lay intertwined, the steamier her memories became. When Dex moved under her touch, she assumed he was merely tilting his head. But the texture of his fur changed too, and the next time she peeked. . .

The panther was gone, and the man was back in its place.

"Gotcha," he whispered, nuzzling her cheek.

She snaked a leg around his thigh and lifted her lips to his. "Got you too."

Which turned out to be the last coherent sentence she uttered for the next few minutes, when the gulping breaths they took had more to do with desire than hard work.

She arched under his touch, then put on the brakes and pointed to a corner of the room.

"Camera."

Dex mumbled, half hidden under her shirt, where he was kissing his way steadily north. "Not sure I care."

She did, though barely, and less so every minute. But she was dirty and sticky with sweat, so. . .

"I bet the shower doesn't have a camera."

Dex stopped long enough to grin. "Good idea. Especially if we turn up the steam."

As it turned out, the two of them generated all the steam needed to throw up a shield against the outside world — especially once they'd stripped, soaped up, and. . .

"Yes. . . " She threw her head back when Dex lifted her against the shower wall and thrust in.

Then he started to rock, and all she could do was wrap her legs around him and hang on.

A damn good thing that shower stall was so big and sturdy. And what bliss to focus exclusively on instinct and pure, raging need, if only for a while.

That was round one. For round two, Dex perched on the triangular seat in a corner of the shower with her pretzeled around him. A position she made a mental note of because, wow. *Penetration* took on a whole new meaning from that angle.

Round three took them to bed — after Dex tossed one towel over the camera and another around the half-hidden mic.

Still, the moment Dakota fell back on the mattress, she stopped and groaned.

"Not working." Not with the mattress sloshing and juggling them around.

Dex pulled her back to her feet. "Time to improvise."

With one sharp tug, he yanked the sheets off the bed. Dakota grabbed the pillows, and soon, they had a nice, cozy nest on the floor. A nest she claimed as her own, taking the top until she was riding her lover like the cowgirl she'd been before going into stunt work.

Destiny.

There it was again — that whisper in her mind. That crazy, confident sensation that everything in her life had led to this very moment, even though she hadn't known it at the time.

Afterward, they lay intertwined — with each other, with the sheets, and even with the thoughts that flitted between their minds like broken-up telegraphs. Just snatches of words and feelings so far, but enough to make her marvel — and feel more certain than ever that Dex was the one.

"Can you really read my mind?"

He nodded. "A little. That's the way it is with mates." He stroked her arm gently, then released a long, shaky breath. "There's one more thing I should tell you."

"Yeah?" she mumbled, still buzzing from the high.

"To be mates... I mean... Well..."

She gave him a stern look. "Dex..."

He hurried to fill in the rest. "Recognizing your mate is one thing. Bonding with her takes..." He swallowed and dropped his eyes to her throat. "There's a kind of... ritual. To seal the deal, I guess."

Her eyebrows shot up as she pictured a cave filled with flickering candles and chanting monks. "A ritual?"

His cheeks showed a hint of pink, and his whisper was so low, she barely heard. "A mating bite."

She frowned. "Sounds like a vampire thing."

He shook his head quickly. "No sucking blood. Just a bite." He drew a hand slowly down her neck. "Right... about... there."

A little shiver went down her spine — the good kind that made all her girl parts tingle and heat.

"No sucking blood," he repeated. "You just hold on, letting your essence mix with hers." Then he shook off the dreamy quality of his voice and added quickly, "And she does the same. When she's ready, I mean."

"What if your mate isn't a shifter? What if she — or he — is human?"

"A shifter can mate with a human. That would make you — I mean, her — a shifter too."

Her eyes went wide. "Seriously?"

He nodded gravely. "Seriously."

She closed her eyes, picturing it. The shifting part was hard to imagine, but prowling around silently on four fleet feet... leaping gracefully between boulders... following scents through the wilderness...

"Doesn't sound too bad," she finally admitted.

"Being a panther is great." Dex flashed a smile, but it faded quickly. "As long as you have space. Another reason to leave Vegas."

She laid a hand over his heart. "You don't have to be a panther to pine for space."

Her eyes wandered over the windowless walls and to the door. How the hell could they escape this mess?

Dex tugged her closer and whispered, "We'll figure something out. I swear."

The sentiment was nice, but crafting watertight plans wasn't one of Dex's strengths. Which meant she'd better get thinking, and fast.

At the same time, cozying up with him was a nice way to escape reality for a little while, so...

She kissed him, setting off a whole new round of fireworks.

Just a little longer, she promised herself, deepening the kiss.

Her body was burning with need, and she couldn't help thinking about what Dex had explained.

A soul mate. The person fate sent you, because you belong together. Forever.

She'd never really believed in such things — but that was before meeting Dex.

His hands slid up her ribs, and she ached for more. But just then, a knock sounded on the door, and they both froze.

Dex groaned, while Dakota tensed. Oh God. Dex had estimated they had forty-eight hours before the fight. What if he was wrong? What if this was it?

They rolled apart, and she pulled on her shirt. Then she grabbed a wooden stool — the nearest "weapon" she could get her hands on — and scurried to one side of the door, signaling for Dex to cover the other.

She shot him a long, hard look, telegraphing, *This could be our chance.*

He nodded back. Then another knock sounded, and they both coiled, ready to fight for their lives.

Chapter Ten

Dex formed a tight fist and called out. "Who is it?"

"Room service," a muffled voice came through the thick door.

He frowned. Was that a trick?

Dakota made a chopping motion with the stool that said, *Whoever it is, when he comes in, you distract him, and I'll bash him over the head. Then we both run like hell.*

He hesitated. He was hardly a master planner, but that sounded pretty sketchy, even to him.

Still, Dakota was Dakota, and you didn't say no. When a key clicked into the lock from the other side, he tensed, ready to act.

"Room service?" he echoed, determined to keep the person's attention on him.

"Special room service." The man outside chuckled.

Dex frowned. Was that a vampire's idea of a joke?

The door swung open, and a steel trolley rolled into view. Half hidden behind the open door, Dakota raised the stool high, ready to smash it over the man's head.

Dex studied the short man in a red uniform and black cap, backed by several burly guards. It really did look like room service.

"Room service supervised by three guards?" he barked, making the situation clear to Dakota.

The room service guy heaved a sigh, though his hat was pulled so low, Dex couldn't see his face. "That's what I said." He fluttered a hand at the guards. "Stand back, boys. I can handle this." Then he raised his chin and winked.

Dex stared. Bob?

He barely bit back the hedgehog shifter's name, waving to Dakota behind his back to stand down.

"Come in." He gestured Bob in, then slammed the door shut on the guards. "It's okay. Just Bob."

Dakota lowered the stool, though her eyes remained fierce.

"Just Bob?" The hedgehog shifter grimaced. "This is what I get for sneaking in to help you — twice?"

Dex shrugged. "Much as I appreciate it, the idea was for us to get out the first time."

Bob waved a hand. "Picky, picky. Now, would you like some lunch?" He raised his voice for the latter part and pushed the trolley toward the table. At the same time, he motioned toward the door, whispering, "We have five minutes, tops. We need to keep this quick."

Dex didn't know what the guy had in mind, but he was all ears. "What do you know? When is the fight?"

Bob started transferring plates of food to the table and lifting lids, making steam and enticing odors waft from each dish. Sweet-and-sour sauce... Roast pork... Thai curry... Dex licked his lips.

"Tomorrow night," Bob said. "The doors open at eight. You're the closing act."

Dex made a face. He didn't like the sound of *closing*, especially when none of it was an act. He and Dakota would be fighting for their lives.

Bob poked him in the chest. "I mean, you." He pulled back the curtain concealing the lower level of the trolley. "I can get your gal out."

Dex stared, as did Dakota. "What?"

Bob waved impatiently to her. "Quick. Get in there, hang on tight, and don't make a sound."

She frowned. "What about Dex?"

Bob looked mournful. Well, he always did. But now, especially so. "It's the best I could do, and you're smaller than Dex. I'm sorry, buddy."

An ache set into Dex's chest, but he forced himself to nod. All that mattered was getting Dakota out unharmed.

"But... But..." Her mouth opened and closed.

Dex took her arm, and Bob fluttered a hand. "Hurry. We don't have much time."

But dammit, Dakota dug in her heels and crossed her arms. "I'm not going. Not without Dex."

His heart skipped a few beats, and for a moment there, he floated on cloud nine. It was only Bob's hiss that brought him back to reality.

"Don't be silly. This is your chance."

Dakota pulled back the curtain, then dropped it. When her hazel eyes met Dex's, he flashed a weak grin. The two of them might be champs when it came to wrapping their bodies around each other, but there was no way they would both fit in that tight space.

Dakota stepped back, shaking her head firmly. "Thanks, but no. Not without Dex."

Bob pursed his lips and tilted his head toward Dex. "I don't suppose you want to. . ."

Dex didn't mean to roar at the poor guy, but that's what his panther side exploded into. "I will never leave my mate!"

Bob cringed. "Okay, okay. No need to get the guards on my case." Then he made a face. "Yeesh. I was just trying to help."

Dex touched his shoulder. "Sorry. I appreciate it. But we need a better plan."

"I wish I had one, buddy. But this is it."

Dex looked at Dakota, ready to beg her to go. But one glance at her blistering expression said, *Fat chance.*

With a sigh, Bob went back to unloading plates. "Well, you might as well enjoy a good meal."

He didn't exactly add, *It could be your last,* but his grim look certainly did.

Dex's mind spun. There had to be some other way out. Meanwhile, Dakota stepped to the table, testing the forks and knives.

"I already checked." Bob shook his head. "They're all plastic. Not much use against the three bears out there and the vampires backing them up."

Dakota's eye went back to the stool, and Dex nearly laughed. Yep, that was Dakota. Resourceful to the last. But not even the roughest, toughest cowgirl could fight her way to freedom with a stool and plastic silverware.

Another knock sounded, and Bob backed the trolley toward the door. "Last chance." Then he slumped at Dakota's stern look. "Okay, okay. I get the message. Pity about the million bucks, though. You want me to donate it to a good cause?"

Dex's mind raced. Any second now, the door would open, and his only contact with the outside world would be gone.

Contact... Outside world... Million bucks...

Dakota's brow furrowed the way it did when she was deep in thought. And most of the time, Dex would take any of her ideas over his own. But Dakota was a good, honest soul, and this was the warped shifter side of Vegas. What the situation called for was a shrewd, all-or-nothing gamble based more on instinct that fact.

"I just wish there was something I could do," Bob lamented, reaching for the doorknob.

And just like that, the answer came to Dex. He shot out a hand, grabbing Bob's sleeve.

"Actually, there is one thing..."

Bob perked up, and Dakota shot Dex a quizzical look.

He closed his eyes for a moment, trying to calculate all the ways his plan could go wrong. But, shoot. There were lots of those, and only the slimmest sliver of hope. Couldn't he do better than that?

Unfortunately, no. He could not. So he gritted his teeth and pulled Bob closer.

"All right. Listen up, and listen good. This is what I need you to do..."

Chapter Eleven

Dex's plan had a major flaw, and Dakota knew it. Hell, they both did, but since she didn't have a better idea...

She sighed and leaned deeper into a stretch, sniffing the fresh floral scent of the tracksuit she'd chosen from the walk-in closet. Twenty-four hours had passed since Bob's visit, and they were down to the last hour before their fight. Would it be the last hour of her life?

She shook off the thought and transitioned to her next stretch. This was just like back in her rodeo days. Thinking about the outcome didn't help — only total concentration on the factors within her control.

Which wasn't a hell of a lot, but she would come out swinging, that was for sure.

"Is this what you did before filming a stunt?" Dex's voice was low and casual. Too casual, really, as he tried to keep things light.

"Yep. With rodeo too. Same stretches every time — more for my mind than my muscles. And then, on movie sets, I would walk through the stunt one last time."

"You want to walk through it again?"

He motioned to the practice gym, but she shook her head. "Not unless you know something I don't know."

They'd been through as many scenarios as they could imagine, but the truth was, they had no idea what to expect. And judging by the intermittent roars of a crowd from somewhere farther along the catacombs, lots of surprises were in store.

Dex shook his head sadly. "I wish I did."

At least there was that. The truth — and respect. Another man might have tried to play tough guy and uttered condescending promises he couldn't keep, but not Dex.

Clank. A key turned in the door lock, and every nerve in her body stood on end.

Dakota forced herself to shoot Dex a firm nod. This was it.

A pair of burly guards shoved the door wide and motioned them out. "One more act, and then you're on. Get moving."

Dakota strode calmly for the door. Part of her was glad to get the waiting over. The other part was... Well, scared.

Dex stepped up behind her, keeping her back covered. Good old Dex, protecting her to the last. It would kill her to see him die trying to defend her, though.

She forced her chin up. *So, make sure it doesn't come to that.*

Grinding the knuckles of one hand into the palm of the other, she put on her best game face. These thugs wanted to see her fight? They would get more than they bargained for.

The roars of the crowd grew louder as the guards ushered her down the long, dark corridor. A second set of guards converged with them, shoving another prisoner forward. Dakota's heart leaped. Was that Bob?

No. It wasn't. Just that annoying vegan vampire, Alon.

"Khloe Maxx. We meet again," he chuckled, mimicking the movie villain in the buildup to the picture's action-packed climax.

She rolled her eyes. How many more times would she have to hear that cheesy line?

Her stomach churned. Probably not too many, given the circumstances.

"Just kidding," Alon mumbled at her icy look.

Dakota stared straight ahead, focusing on any clues regarding the upcoming fight.

A set of heavy doors swung open before them, and the corridor grew wider. Other corridors joined in from the sides, and lights shone from around a bend ahead.

"The arena," Alon whispered.

Dakota might as well have been a time traveler visiting the Colosseum in Rome. Somewhere above, a crowd sat in stone bleachers. The noise grew to a din, and dust showered from overhead as hundreds of feet stomped in unison. Here and there, the sand-strewn floor was streaked with dark marks. Blood? Dakota shivered, picturing limp bodies being pulled from the arena one at a time.

A massive pair of reinforced doors loomed ahead. Light filtered in around the edges along with the deafening sound of the crowd. Dakota took a deep breath, trying to settle her pulse.

"Wait there." One of the guards motioned to an alcove on the right. "Don't move."

She hesitated, then stepped into the small space. Dex pressed in next, creating a wall between her and her captors. Alon was the last to shuffle in.

He cast a quick glance over his shoulder, then leaned in to whisper. "I'll make you a deal."

Dex shook his head, looking more menacing than ever.

"I don't make deals with vampires."

Alon snorted. "No, only with bear shifters who skip town before you can. Any regrets?"

Dakota froze at the dig at Dex's friend Tanner, who had masterminded the evening that had led to all this.

Dex started to shake his head, then stopped, looking at her. "Regrets? Only one. Getting Dakota involved."

Her heart warmed but, damn. Dex looked so pained. Did he really think their chances were so small?

Alon snorted. "How very noble. Still, that won't get either of you out alive."

"And you can?" Dakota countered.

Alon shook his head. "Sorry, honey. But you know what? I think you two have a slim chance of getting out of here alive. Still, you don't have what I have."

"Which is?" she prompted.

Alon raised his chin. "The means to bring down these bloodsuckers forever."

Dex rolled his eyes. "Says one vampire about another."

"I'm not like them." Sparks practically flew from Alon's eyes.

Dakota put a hand on Dex's arm and locked eyes with Alon. "What are you saying?"

"I'm saying, we work together. Getting out of here alive isn't enough. Not if we want to stop Schiller for good."

Dex fanned a finger back and forth. "There is no *we* here."

"There could be," Alon insisted. "Think of the next innocent victim, and the next, and the next..."

"The next guy can take care of himself," Dex grumbled.

Alon made a face. "Khloe Maxx wouldn't say that."

"She's not Khloe Maxx!" Dex roared.

Dakota bit her lip. As much as she hated the association with the skimpy outfit and stale lines, another aspect of the action heroine appealed. The courage. The willingness to step up and right wrongs.

But Dex was right, too, as he railed on. "That was a movie, you get it? Fiction. Hollywood. Make-believe."

Dakota gulped hard. Yes, it was. Was she crazy to even think about taking a stand — against vampires?

Still, a little twitch set in beside her eye, because every time an adoring fan mistook her for a hero, she felt like a con.

Alon kept his eyes on hers. "Even ordinary people can be heroic sometimes."

Dakota's heart thumped a little harder. Maybe Alon was right. Maybe this was her chance to shine.

Then again... Well, Dex did have a point.

She nearly laughed at herself there. Usually, she was the practical one. Dex was the dreamer. Yet here they were in reversed roles.

She swallowed hard. "What exactly do you have in mind?"

Dex stuck his arm between them. "You are not doing this, Dakota. We have to focus on getting out of here alive."

She pursed her lips. "All I'm saying is, let's hear him out."

Alon's eyes sparkled, and he clapped his hands. "Right. Remember when Khloe Maxx fought the dastardly overlord Harkonnen?"

When he gushed on, reliving every sword swing in that film — and others — Dakota lost hope. Maybe Dex was right. It was time to be practical, not heroic.

She put up a hand to break into Alon's excited babble. "This is not the time—"

He cut her off. "On the contrary, I think it is. Remember the uprising in *Spartacus Revamped?* You beat all those zombies."

"Fake zombies." Dex jerked a thumb toward the arena. "What's in there is real. All of it."

"True, but I have faith in you two. And I swear, if you help me, I will bury Schiller and his goons for good." Then Alon winked. "Also, I know what awaits us in there. And as a wise aardvark once said, knowledge is power."

Dex lifted the vampire and pushed him against the wall. "Then tell us what you know. Now."

Alon's feet dangled an inch above the sandy floor. Still, he shook his head. "Only if you promise to get me out of there with you."

Dex's eyes shone with fury, but Dakota squeezed his shoulder, communicating, *This could be our chance.*

He could be lying. Dex's furious eyes flashed.

Dakota considered. Yes, Alon could be lying. Still, when she thought about what Bernie, the arena manager, had said...

Death around every corner... Close calls... Dripping blood...

She locked eyes with Dex. They needed all the help they could get.

"You help me, I help you." Alon wiggled under Dex's tight grasp. "And together, we can shut down Schiller forever."

Dakota took a deep breath, then made up her mind. When she signaled Dex, he grimaced, then dropped Alon like a slippery fish. When the vampire fell to his ass in the sand, Dex loomed over him, glaring.

"All right, then. Tell us."

Alon wobbled awkwardly to his feet. Then he motioned them both closer and rubbed his hands. "Okay. Listen closely. We don't have much time."

Chapter Twelve

"It's showtime. Move it." A guard motioned Dex gruffly toward the oak door, then turned to Dakota. "You too, sweetheart."

Dex all but bared his teeth. *She's not your sweetheart, asshole. She's mine.*

Dakota, as always, remained perfectly composed, her eyes fixed firmly on the doors. Alon cowered right behind her, the little rat.

The question was, did the little rat tell the truth? Dex's panther growled.

An announcer's voice boomed through the thick doors, and the crowd went wild.

"Ladies and gentlemen, thank you for your patience as we set up the grand finale. And now..." The announcer drew out the word, letting anticipation build. "The time has come! Sit back, relax, and enjoy as the Scarlet Palace presents the finale you've all been waiting for!"

The light filtering around the edges of the doors flickered, and the crowd cheered.

To Dex's left, backstage workers hustled a wooden contraption into the arena through a side door. Unfortunately, he couldn't see much from his angle — just the darkness beyond, punctuated by a sweeping spotlight.

He ground his teeth. It felt like an eternity since the previous "act" had been ushered offstage — a furious rhino shifter with a blood-stained horn, followed by a frighteningly limp body dragged by two orderlies. Then the backstage crew had swept through, setting up some kind of elaborate set.

"Just as I said," Alon whispered as a giant bladed contraption was trundled past.

Dex stared at it, wide-eyed. When Alon had first revealed what to expect, Dex had had his doubts. But maybe the vampire hadn't been bullshitting after all.

"Without further ado...." the announcer boomed, only to pause again.

Dakota stirred the air with her hand. "That's *with* further ado, asshole."

Dex let a growl build in his throat, ready to protect his mate at all costs. Or rather, he clacked his fangs, having already shifted to panther form.

The good news was that Dakota had barely batted an eye when he'd shifted. Well, okay — maybe she'd gone stiff for a while. But other than that, she'd turned steadfastly forward, muttering, "We got this."

His heart warmed. His mate was the most amazing woman in the world.

Then his shoulders tensed, and he lashed his tail. Whatever happened, she had to survive.

The announcer hollered, working the crowd into a frenzy. "The Scarlet Palace brings you the black panther, the warrior princess, and the buffoon!"

The massive doors flew open, and they were bathed in blinding white light. Dex squinted, while Dakota held up a hand.

Alon cursed. "The buffoon?"

The crowd hooted as the announcer went on. "Who — if anyone — will survive the ultimate test? Who will be the first to fall?"

Dex gritted his teeth. *Not me,* he vowed. *Not Dakota.*

None of us, Dakota reminded him with a stern look. Then she strode forward, keeping her chin up.

The spotlight inched forward with them, and Dex stared into the darkness beyond.

"Ladies and gentlemen, feast your eyes on Las Vegas's latest, greatest, and deadliest new show — the Pit of Doom!"

Dakota rolled her eyes. "Sounds like another bad movie."

The spotlight jumped into a frenzy, much like the crowd. The piercing light swept from side to side, revealing snippets of a sinister whole. Dex squinted, catching glimpses of walls, ropes, and... crocodiles? Then a strobe light came on, illuminating the arena in painfully short bursts.

"Just like I said," Alon sniffed, barely audible above the crowd's wild cheers. "An obstacle course."

"Whoa," Dakota muttered,

Dex stared. *Whoa* was right. The Pits were known for gladiator-style fights, but this was more, combining fights with deadly obstacles.

He prowled forward, ready to repel whatever came hurtling at them. Dakota yanked a sword and shield off a rack on their right, then hissed at Alon to do the same.

"Helmet," she added, slipping one on.

Alon's eyes went wide. "I hate to say it, but you really do look like Khloe Maxx."

She grimaced, swinging her sword. "You want my help? Then don't piss me off."

When she turned away, Alon hid a grin, and it occurred to Dex that the vampire might be right. Getting riled up might be just what Dakota needed to survive the challenges ahead.

"Last call to place your bets, ladies and gentlemen. Last call," the announcer boomed.

"That's right," Alon murmured. "Place your bets. Especially you, asshole." His eyes shot daggers at a figure in the VIP balcony that jutted out from the stands above.

"Schiller." Dakota cursed. Then she shot Alon a look that said, *This had better work.*

Dex gnashed his teeth, not sure it would. But for now, he would concentrate on the *survival* aspect of their plan.

"You, dear audience, are the real winners today," the announcer continued. "But in the unlikely event that any of our contestants survives the three rounds, he or she will win their choice of a luxury condominium in Scarlet Towers or a million dollars!"

"I'll show you *unlikely*," Dakota growled, defiant as ever.

As the announcer droned on with a long-winded plug for vacation properties in Scarlet Towers, Dex pressed against Dakota's legs, hoping it communicated what he felt. That he would be there for her, no matter what. That somehow, they would get through this.

Then a bell rang, and the spotlights converged on an unusual structure. "Ladies and gentlemen, our first obstacle — the Pit of Death!"

A guard prodded them with a pike. "Go."

Dex prowled forward, leading the way up a short wooden ramp. The crowd broke into a rhythmic chant accompanied by two claps, then a stomp.

"Pit of Death! Pit of Death!"

"More like the swamp of death," Dakota sniffed.

Twenty crocodiles lay in a mud pit at least fifteen yards across, all clacking their jaws.

"Like this?" Alon reached for one of the Tarzan-style ropes dangling from above.

Dex looked up as Dakota gave it a sharp tug, then shook her head. "It's rigged to break. See that joint up there?"

He snarled as Alon grumbled. "Schiller's playing dirty. Why am I not surprised?"

With a sharp creak, the ramp underfoot began to lift — and lift, tipping them toward the morass. Alon stumbled into Dakota. "Help!"

Clap-clap-stomp. Clap-clap-stomp. "Pit of Death! Pit of Death!" the crowd thundered.

"Go!" Dakota shooed Dex forward. Then she turned to Alon. "Think of them as stepping-stones. And whatever you do, keep moving!"

Dex eyed the crocodiles, then leaped. As a feline, he was confident of getting across. But, hell. What about Dakota?

The crocodile he landed on first heaved and snapped, but Dex was too quick. In a flash, he jumped to the next beast, and the next... All the way over to the platform on the other side. He leaped onto it, safe and sound, then spun around.

The crowd broke into applause because, wow. Dakota was only one step behind him. Man, was she quick. But Alon...

94

"Black panther and the warrior princess are across!" the announced boomed. "But the crocodiles smell blood, and I do too!"

He meant Alon, who was still teetering on the first crocodile, while the others slowly converged.

"Keep moving!" Dakota yelled.

Dex lashed his tail against her legs, making his message clear.

Forget him. They couldn't afford to wait for Alon.

But Dakota gripped her sword harder and leaped back out onto the nearest crocodile's back. The crowd roared, and the announcer did too.

"And the warrior princess heads back!"

Dex rumbled helplessly. Was she nuts?

Maybe, but she was damn agile too, leaping from one crocodile to another, all the way over to Alon. The crocodiles turned for Dakota, lightning-fast. But she was just as fast — and fearless, bashing them with her shield and sword.

"Move it!" she barked at Alon. "Now!"

Dex had no choice but to dash back, drawing some of the crocodiles' attention away. One nearly snapped off his hind foot, but he jumped away just in time.

"Dex!" Dakota yelled once she and Alon were safely across.

With a mighty heave of his back legs, Dex sailed over the last three crocodiles and landed beside Dakota with a thump.

The crowd exploded into cheers, and Alon grinned. "We did it!"

Dex snarled. *Dakota and I did it. You were nearly crocodile kibble, man.*

Alon pointed ahead. "You help me, I help you, remember?"

Dex found it hard to imagine Alon contributing much. But by then, the ramp was tipping again, forcing them toward the next obstacle. Two bare-chested gladiators stood before it, swinging clubs.

"Step aside, asshole," Dakota grunted, driving back the one on the right.

Dex snarled at the one on the left.

Clang! Dakota's sword struck the first gladiator's helmet.

Whack! Dex smacked the other's ribs with a paw.

Within seconds, both gladiators backed away, staring at Dakota in fear and surprise.

Dex nearly grinned. That was his mate, all right.

"Our contestants might have survived the Pit of Death. . ." the announcer chimed in. "But will they get around the Night Crawl?"

The spectators jeered, cheered, and munched popcorn. Dex growled in their direction, then froze. Among the sea of frenzied faces yelling for blood was one perfectly still figure, his face obscured by a deep hood. Someone waiting. . . watching. . . For what?

But there was no time to puzzle that out, because three dark shapes came zooming through the air, heading right for him.

"Hit the floor!" Dakota shoved Alon down.

Dex crouched, then snapped as the flying beast hurtled by. What the hell?

"Those vultures are hungry, folks," the announcer cackled.

"Vultures, my ass," Alon grunted. "Those are gargoyles."

Dex frowned, watching the winged beasts circle for another pass. Alon was right. Those were gargoyles — nasty, twisted creatures the size of a small pterosaur, armed with curved beaks and sharp claws. But magic hung in the air, thanks to three witches sitting in a booth high above. In between knitting, the trio wiggled their fingers and murmured spells to cloak any supernatural elements from the humans in the audience. Even vampires like Schiller knew better than to reveal too much.

"Under there," Dakota pushed Alon toward an area covered by low-strung barbed wire. "Use your elbows. Like this. . ."

And off she went, crawling like a commando under enemy fire.

"Oh! Oh! You did this in *Troops of Dawn,* didn't you?" Alon gushed.

Dakota snorted. "Yeah. Without the gargoyles."

Dex nearly crouched and raced under the barbed wire with them. But with the gargoyles racing in for another pass, he jumped up instead, balancing on the wooden posts that supported the barbed wire.

"Help!" Alon cried as a gargoyle dive-bombed him, clacking its claws.

Dakota stuck her sword through a gap in the barbed wire, repelling the screeching beast. Meanwhile, Dex swiped at the nearest gargoyle's wing, shredding it with his claws. The creature screamed and smashed into the barbed wire, where it hung, tangled and cursing.

The crowd cheered again, and Dex spotted Dakota racing ahead. When she popped out on the far side of the field, she ran straight for a wall of weapons, then whirled and threw something.

"Duck!" she yelled.

Dex crouched just in time for something to whiz past his ear. It spun onward, striking the gargoyle behind him. The creature yelped and flew off, clawing at an object impaled in its ribs. A barbed star?

"Just like in *Dawn of the Ninja*." Alon beamed.

Dex stared. Dakota knew martial arts too?

The crowd cheered wildly, putting new words to their *clap-clap-stomp* tune. "Khlo-ee Maxx! Khlo-ee Maxx!"

"Come on!" Dakota pulled Alon to his feet.

After a last snarl of warning, Dex leaped over to join them. By then, two gargoyles were tangled helplessly in the barbed wire, and the third flew off to roost at a safe distance.

"Third-rate gargoyles," a woman muttered from the nearest row of seats. "Not to mention those witches..."

Dex snapped his head around. Why did she sound familiar?

But he couldn't make out a face in the blur of that crowd. And with a final obstacle coming up, he didn't have a moment to spare. Especially with a side door opening and a pack of wolves racing out, baying for blood. They all converged on Dex, Dakota, and Alon, then slowed, driving the trio toward the final obstacle.

Dex dragged his eyes away from the wolves long enough to glance ahead, where a twenty-foot flame shot out from a niche in the wall.

Whoosh! The scent of sulfur hit him, and he wrinkled his nose.

"Dragon," Alon muttered.

Dakota stopped in her tracks. "You're kidding, right?"

Dex looked to the right. No, Alon wasn't kidding. There really was a dragon shooting flames out from behind a flimsy, camouflaged wall. To human eyes, it would look like a flamethrower, but to Dex...

He forced a gulp down his dry throat. The wolves kept advancing. On either side, stone walls funneled them into a space where they would be sitting ducks to the dragon. A panther might survive all manner of shifter attacks. But no cat in the world, no matter how courageous, had a chance against a dragon.

He glanced desperately at Dakota. She held up her shield bravely, but it would incinerate in seconds, and then—

Dex cut off the thought, desperate for some other way out. But what?

Chapter Thirteen

Dakota shot Dex a desperate look. So far, they'd managed to sneak past every obstacle. But, crap. A fire-breathing dragon?

Alon straightened his shirt and marched forward. "Leave this to me, honey."

She grabbed his arm. "Are you insane?"

Alon turned with a grin. "Like I said, you help me, I help you."

"And now, the next obstacle — Dragon Fire!" the announcer crowed.

Literally. Dakota bit her lip as she, Dex, and Alon were forced forward into the ever-narrower space.

"Dra-gon fire! Dra-gon fire!" the crowd thundered, keeping up that clapping, stomping beat.

Dakota held her shield tightly. Was Alon bluffing, or did he actually have a trick up his sleeve?

She shot Dex a glance, marveling at his sleek, feline body for the umpteenth time. A body he'd thrown into danger again and again — for her. If they made it through this—

When we make it through this, she corrected herself.

—she would never, ever doubt love again. But first...

She took a deep breath and forced herself to follow Alon. Here she went, breaking a cardinal rule of her stunt career — to never, ever cede control to anyone, especially if that person had yet to prove himself. But now, she had no choice. Not with a pack of wolves snapping at her heels.

She swung her sword at the nearest two, who scuttled back.

"Stay close." Alon stuck out his left elbow. "I can only gain us so much space."

Dakota threaded her arm through his elbow and pressed close to his side. Dex growled and stuck his head between them, but Alon pushed him back.

"Not trying to steal your girl, buddy. Just trying to get her through this alive, all right?"

Dex grumbled but gave in, winding around Dakota's free side. She lowered a hand to the silky fur of his back, and off they went like Dorothy and her friends on their way to Oz.

"When I say *now*, shut your eyes and hold your breath. And keep close."

Dakota's stomach flipped when a low rasp came from the right. The dragon was sucking in a breath, ready to spit fire. Then came a terrifying moment of silence, and a split second later—

Whoosh! A huge flame erupted from the right, drowning out the noise of the crowd.

"Now!" Alon barked, throwing up his free hand to block the flames.

As it turned out, closing your eyes and holding your breath were an instinctive reaction to being bathed in flames. Dakota gritted her teeth as heat and wind raged all around.

Wait. Not wind, she realized. That was the force of the dragon's breath.

Alon lurched into her side, and she pushed back. Whatever he was doing, it was working — so far. She wasn't about to let him stumble now.

Every step was like wading through quicksand, and every beat of her heart felt like her last. Dakota dug her fingers into Dex's thick pelt. Time seemed to slow down, and she was running out of air. If they didn't step out of the dragon's fire soon...

Alon took one more step, then stumbled, dragging her down. Her eyes flew open, and she cursed. God, this was it. She was going to die.

But the whoosh of the fire was drowned out by the rabid cheer of the crowd. Dex yowled, and somehow, Dakota knew to interpret that as, *Hurry up!*

100

Propping Alon up, she hurried forward, out of the dragon's line of fire. Then she stood, panting and checking her friends. Had they really made it through unscathed?

Not quite. Alon shook, cradling his right arm. Wisps of smoke slipped out from between his fingers, and she was afraid to take a closer look. Still, they were alive! Apparently, vampires had the ability to withstand a dragon's flames — at least for a limited time.

"You did it!" she cheered.

Alon flashed a huge smile. "I did, didn't I?"

Dakota crouched down and threw her arms around Dex. "We did it! We really did it!"

The joy and relief surging through her doubled when Dex nuzzled her with his velvety cheek. His whiskers tickled her skin, and she giggled. "That feels so good. I could get into this panther thing."

In more ways than one, a little voice in the back of her mind hummed when she remembered what Dex had said.

A shifter can mate with a human. That would make her a shifter too.

The more she thought about it, the more she liked the idea. But first, they had to get out of this hellhole.

She straightened, grinning at the crowd's cheers. "Let's see — do I want the luxury condominium in Scarlet Towers or a million dollars?"

She was joking, of course, but Alon looked dead serious. "Even as a vegan, I know better than to count my chickens before they hatch."

Dakota frowned. "What do you mean? The announcer said..."

Alon pinned her with a look that made her trail off. Crap. He was right. Just because Schiller promised something didn't mean he would actually go through with it.

At exactly that moment, the announcer came on the air again.

"What a show, ladies and gentlemen. What a show! There's just one more obstacle for our contestants to face. Something guaranteed to spill blood."

101

Everyone cheered, and Dakota's shoulders drooped. Of course, Schiller wasn't going to let them out alive. How could she have been so naïve?

Dex prowled toward the VIP box and snarled, but Schiller just waved.

Don't you see, you fool? the vampire's haughty expression said. *I win. I always win. And you lose.*

Dakota brought her sword arm back, judging the distance. In *The Rough and the Ruthless*, she'd thrown a sword end over end to pin one of the bad guys to a wall in a grisly scene audiences loved. She'd practiced that move so many times, she could pull it off in her sleep. But this sword was double the weight of her Hollywood prop, and Schiller was twice as far away.

Besides, doors flew open on all sides of the arena just then, and a slew of gladiators strode in. Ten, at least, plus several wolves who released bloodcurdling howls. Worse, the statues decorating the arena came to life, and a dozen gargoyles emerged from solid stone, ready to pounce.

The audience went wild, as did the announcer. "History buffs can consult their programs for full details on each of our gladiators, from the Thracian to the Retiarii, the Samnite, and more!"

Dakota rocked her jaw from side to side, doing her best to steady her nerves. But, hell. Death was a tricky thing to face, especially in an arena packed with bloodthirsty fans cheering it on. Schiller might as well have thrown a Grim Reaper-themed fighter with a scythe into the mix.

"Stand back-to-back," she ordered the others as she searched for some means of escape. A trap door in the arena floor? A ladder dangling from a helicopter that appeared just in the nick of time?

Too bad those were all movie stunts, and this was the real thing.

Dex and Alon pressed in, and they turned as one when the gladiators closed in. Blades glinted in the spotlights, and the wolves howled for blood. Dakota bashed her spear against her shield, refusing to show fear. But inside... Her stomach flipped. This was it. The end.

Then Dex whipped his head around, staring at a section of the crowd.

Dakota followed his gaze, spotting a man running toward the arena. "Now what?"

Dex let out a low chuff of hope. Why?

The man took the bleacher stairs three at a time, throwing back a cloak as he went. Then he shifted into wolf form in mid-step and leaped to the arena floor.

Alon shook his head bitterly. "As if the gladiators aren't enough..."

Another man followed suit from the opposite side. He charged forward, barreling past two guards and into the arena as he shifted into bear form.

Dakota's knees shook as the wolf and bear charged past the gladiators, coming straight for her. But at the last possible second, the beasts spun around and snarled at the surrounding men.

Dex made the strangest sound — one she swore said, *Boy, am I glad to see you guys.* What was going on?

A moment later, all hell broke loose. Gargoyles swooped overhead while swords swung and beasts snarled. Dakota found herself facing two gladiators armed with tridents.

"Damn Retiarii," she muttered, warding them off with her shield.

"Help!" Alon yelled as a wolf jumped for his throat.

Dakota smacked the beast's hindquarters with her sword, then spun back to the gladiators.

Behind them, Dex tackled another foe. The wolf and bear that had rushed down from the stands fought just as fiercely, helping Dex. Who they were, Dakota had no idea. But, heck. She would take all the help she could get.

Still, it was a melee, and she was right in the thick of it. Using every trick she knew, she fought for her life. And frankly, she was doing pretty damn well. But for every gladiator she pushed away or wild beast she dodged, two others pressed in.

It was only a matter of time before she succumbed to the overwhelming number of foes.

When a sword nicked her upper arm, she cried out. The next gladiator knocked her shield sideways, wrenching her wrist. Dex snarled, trying to fight his way closer to her, but another gladiator blocked his way.

"Help!" Alon cried.

Dakota spun around and kicked at the wolf that had pinned him to the ground. Then she pulled Alon to his feet and—

"Oh!" He pointed behind her.

She flinched, sure it was a gladiator ready to skewer her with his sword. But when she turned, she spotted a woman running through the surrounding crowd, yelling, "Schiller, you liar! You cheat!"

Dakota scanned the crowd. Who was that?

Even the gladiators turned to stare as the woman ran to the top of the risers and spread her arms. A shimmer appeared around her body, and the audience gasped.

"All part of the show, ladies and gents. All part of the show," the announcer said, none too convincingly.

Three security men rushed at the woman, but she merely closed her eyes, tipped her chin up, and bent her knees.

"Oh my God, she's going to jump!" someone screamed.

As it turned out, it was more of a soaring dive. Make that, a glide. Make that—

Dakota stared. A flight? Because the woman wasn't a woman any more. She was a dragon, swooping over the arena.

The audience broke into confused cries. The nearest wolf — the dark one who appeared to be Dex's friend — yipped proudly and wagged his tail. Meanwhile, the gladiators either raised their weapons in defense or retreated toward the arena doors.

"Get her, you cowards!" Schiller yelled from his VIP seat. Then he ducked for cover as the dragon spat a ten-foot flame at him.

Dakota stared. What was going on?

"Wow. Best special effects I've ever seen," the nearest audience member marveled.

Dakota gulped. If only he knew.

"Ladies and gentlemen..." the announcer started. But a crash sounded behind him, and his next words were aimed at someone else. "You can't come in here, miss. This is off-limits."

"I'll show you off-limits, asshole," a woman grumbled in the background.

Then a tussle broke out, and the audience peered up in alarm. Finally, someone snatched up the microphone, and a woman's voice boomed over the arena.

"Ladies and gentlemen, this is Officer Proulx of the Las Vegas Fire Commission."

Dakota frowned. Fire Commission?

"We regret to inform you that we've detected a fire hazard," the woman went on.

Dakota stared at the dragon circling overhead. Was it grinning?

"I repeat, a fire hazard," the woman said into the mic. "We'll need everyone to evacuate in an orderly manner. And whatever you do, don't panic."

She emphasized *panic*, prompting half the crowd to do exactly that.

"Oh, and don't forget to claim your winnings on the way out," the woman chuckled. "The managers of the Scarlet Palace have assured us they will honor every claim, as well as refunding all tickets in full."

"Refunding *what?*" Schiller yelped. The dragon turned back toward him, and he ducked for cover again.

"Bye, everyone, and have a nice day," the new announcer chuckled.

Dakota stared as the audience streamed frantically for the exits. One bald, portly man ambled, though, flashing Dex a sly smile. Was that Bob?

Alon took her elbow and steered her toward a side door. "I think that's our cue to exit stage right." He waved at the gladiators huddled in the archway. "Out of the way, I say. Out of the way! Warrior princess coming through."

For the first time ever, Dakota felt the part — especially when the gladiators hurried aside. Of course, it didn't hurt to have three ferocious carnivores at her side — a panther, a wolf, and a bear, not to mention a dragon crowding into the tight space from behind. Every living soul fled, leaving the wide corridor to Dakota and her allies. Hot air whooshed out from behind as the dragon daintily folded its wings and shifted to human form, grabbing a robe from the gladiators' area.

"Hi. I'm Kaya. And that's Trey." Grinning, the woman pointed to the wolf, then offered her hand. "Nice to meet you."

Dakota shook, a little awed. "Nice to meet you."

Alon rubbed his hands in glee and motioned to a side corridor. "Well, I'll be off. I have a bet to collect. Nice working with you."

Dakota managed a little wave as Dex, still in panther form, butted against her legs, steering her in a different direction. Whoa. Was she really bidding a vampire goodbye? And yikes — was the cavalry who'd come to her rescue really a trio of shifters?

"That's Tanner," Kaya pointed to the bear. "And that's my sister Karen up in the announcer's booth."

Dakota blinked. "Your sister?"

Kaya grinned. "I promise, I'll explain. But let's get out of here first. Oh, with a quick stop to collect our winning bets on the way."

Chapter Fourteen

One week later...

Dakota sat on the top step of the cabin, gazing toward the Wind River Mountains. A week had passed since the fight in the Scarlet Palace, and she was only starting to breathe freely now. Dex was at her side, and he bumped his shoulder gently against hers.

"Not a bad view, huh?"

She broke into a huge smile. "Sure beats Las Vegas."

His grin matched hers. "Everything here beats Vegas. Of course, the cabin can use some upgrades..."

He gestured over his shoulder at the slope-roofed structure, one of several on Flying Aces Ranch.

She laughed. Yeah, the cabin was definitely a fixer-upper. But, hey. The stone fireplace and cedar beams were stunning, not to mention the views. And anyway, she was still counting her luck, from surviving the fighting pits of the Scarlet Palace to this opportunity — an invitation to live and work in Wyoming. A beautiful place with great people — starting with the owners of the ranch.

"It does need fixing up," she agreed. "But that will be fun. Our own place..."

And there it was again — another of those *Pinch me, I'm dreaming* moments.

Kaya, the dragon shifter, came sauntering around the corner of the house — in human form, thank goodness. "Dinner's ready. Are you?"

Dex practically jumped to his feet. "Yes, ma'am."

Dakota followed with a chuckle. Dex had been out prowling the forest in panther form for most of the previous night, followed by catnapping for most of the day. That and making slow, sweet love to her in the cozy little cabin they'd been assigned, set slightly apart from the other ranch buildings.

The tiny scar on her neck tingled and warmed, marking the spot where Dex had placed his mating bite. Soon, she would be able to shift into panther form too, and she couldn't wait. According to Dex, the process took anywhere from a few days to weeks, and she was eager to experience it for herself. But for now...

A voice growled in the back of her mind. *Dinner. Need food.*

She might not have shifted yet, but her panther side was gradually emerging in more subtle ways.

"Nice, huh?" Kaya motioned to the mountains.

"It's gorgeous," Dakota agreed. "And it was all your grandfather's?"

Kaya nodded. "All three thousand acres, but no one has worked the ranch in years. That's why we're so glad to have your help."

We were Kaya and her sister, Karen, a dragon-witch mix, who'd jointly inherited the ranch. Living there with them were their mates — Trey, a wolf shifter, and Tanner, the bear who had set off the chain of events that led to Dakota and Dex coming to Wyoming for a fresh start. Dex had explained the whole story to Dakota, and Kaya and Karen had filled in the details over crackling bonfires during the past several evenings — evenings full of laughter, chatter, and friendly banter.

Never thought I'd find my mate in a casino, but there he was, Kaya, the she-dragon, had chuckled, reeling Trey in for a hug.

And man, the trouble we got into together, Trey had half sighed, half laughed. *But, hey. We got out of it again, right?*

My trouble started with stealing a diamond, Karen had laughed. *Maybe not my best plan...*

Plan? What plan? Tanner had sighed.

108

Karen had play-smacked his thick arm. *Hey, it turned out well, right?*

Dakota grinned. There had been times when she'd cursed Tanner for getting Dex involved in a money-grabbing scheme at the Scarlet Palace. But now that she'd experienced the full extent of Schiller's evil firsthand, she understood how justified it was.

Besides, Tanner wasn't to blame. It was destiny, ushering each couple through their own trials and tribulations until they'd all found their happily-ever-afters in this wonderful place.

Dakota let out a happy sigh. Great place, great people — er, shifters — and a great new job.

"I'm dying to get to work," she told Kaya. "And so is Thunder."

She motioned to the pretty mare grazing in a nearby paddock — a roan, her favorite color. And, yes — her very own horse, purchased with her own money. Another dream had come true. The folks at the neighboring ranch might not have seen the horse's potential, but Dakota did.

Kaya grinned. "Starting Monday. You have a whole weekend left."

"Really, I wouldn't mind..."

Kaya shook her head. "When Trey and I first arrived here from Las Vegas, we needed a little time to decompress. I figure you and Dex could use that too." Then she winked. "Besides, I'm sure you'll find ways to pass the next two days."

Dakota hid a grin while that voice hummed inside. *Oh, I'm sure we will.*

Her cheeks flushed as she brushed against Dex. It was crazy, the animal instincts he set off in her.

At the same time, she truly did look forward to her new job as head wrangler at Flying Aces Ranch. Her dream job, with most of the day spent outdoors and in the saddle, herding cattle or training horses. No more stunt work and, hopefully, no more vampires. Ever.

Dex, meanwhile, would take advantage of his panther form to hunt down cattle that strayed into hard-to-reach territory,

ANNA LOWE

and he would also give Tanner a hand with his new reclaimed lumber business.

Dakota took a deep breath. It was perfect — all of it. And so peaceful. Horses quietly grazing in a nearby paddock, a mountain stream gurgling beside the winding path. The rustle of aspen leaves and the golden glow that heralded the end of another beautiful day.

A scene that couldn't possibly be more perfect, except it was, what with the scent of sizzling steaks drawing them ahead.

"Perfect timing." Karen waved as they approached the terrace beside her home. "Tanner says the steaks are done."

"Nearly done," the bear shifter corrected, raising a hand in greeting.

Dakota added a potato salad to the side dishes already filling the table, and Trey offered drinks.

"Bitterroot Brewery IPA. Okay with you? Recommended by my cousin's friends — the bear shifters who run the Blue Moon Saloon."

Kaya chuckled. "Trey and I drove down to visit his cousin on Twin Moon Ranch, and they sent us over to the saloon. That place is definitely the real deal."

Dakota hid a smile. Bear shifters who ran a saloon? Wolf shifters who operated a huge ranch? Dex had introduced her to a whole new world she'd never known about, and she couldn't wait to see those places for herself. Maybe someday, when things settled down here...

As much as the thought appealed, she filed it away for another day. She had plenty to discover here first.

Starting with that steak, her inner beast hummed.

Dinner was delicious, and the good company made time fly. The sun set, and the stars emerged, creating a grandiose backdrop to the crackling fire Tanner got going in the outdoor hearth.

"Wow. This is perfect." Dakota reached for Dex's hand. "Instead of neon lights, we have stars. And instead of honking traffic, we have crickets." She closed her eyes, listening for a moment. "Not to mention the nice temperature..."

110

"It is perfect here in summer. But in winter..." Karen sighed. "Well, it's beautiful in winter too. So, really, it's just mud season you have to endure."

"Not tempted to head back to Vegas, are you?" Trey joked.

Karen snorted. "Never again. Not when I've got everything I need right here." She leaned against Tanner's massive shoulder. But a moment later, she fluttered her hands and jumped to her feet. "Oh, that reminds me. Did you hear this?"

She strode over to the porch, grabbed a tablet, and scrolled down. "From today's *Las Vegas Review-Journal...*" She cleared her throat and started to read. "*Owners of Westend Casino announce renovations at Vegas gun range.*"

Everyone cheered, and Dakota gave a little fist pump. Yes, she'd finally found a buyer for her share of Hot Shots. What a relief to have that off her hands — and the cash in her account.

"Westend Casino?" Kaya leaned in for a look.

"The one and only," Trey sighed. When Dakota tilted her head, he explained. "Westend Casino is owned by the Westend wolf pack. We paid them an unintended visit not too long ago..."

He shot Kaya a wry smile, and she rolled her eyes. "Don't remind me."

"More shifters?" Dakota asked.

"What can I say? Vegas is full of them. None particularly friendly."

"Well, I'm just glad to be rid of the gun range," Dakota decided. "And who knows? I might find a ranch of my own around here to invest the money in."

"Just don't go leaving us," Kaya threw in. "We need you."

Dakota laughed. "Not going anywhere, believe me."

"That was from the business section." Karen went back to reading. "Here's an article on the front page. Ready?"

When everyone nodded, she started.

"*Shake-up at Scarlet Enterprises: New Investors, New Board Members, New Management. New Direction?*" Her eyes sparkled. "That's the headline. Check out the picture. Recognize anyone?"

111

She turned the device around, flashing the side-by-side images on the title page.

Dakota groaned. "Igor Schiller? And, whoa. Is that Alon?"

"Barely recognized him in the business suit," Dex murmured.

Karen grinned and went back to reading. "*According to the latest press release, Scarlet Enterprises welcomes its newest board member: vegan activist Alon Edgar. 'We are delighted to welcome Mr. Edgar and his visionary team to lead Scarlet Palace through an exciting new phase of development,' spokesperson Mandy Sangre said.*"

Kaya cackled. "Igor doesn't look delighted."

Karen's grin grew wider. "That's the best part. *Igor Schiller, long-standing CEO, has announced a lateral move to his place of birth in Romania's Transylvania region. 'It's time I get back to my roots and spend more time with my family,' Mr. Schiller was reported to say.*" Karen snorted. "Yeah, right."

Everyone laughed, and Dex made a show of rubbing his chin. "Now, where did Alon get the cash to buy a controlling share of Scarlet Enterprises?"

Tanner humpfed. "Yeah, I wonder. A well-placed bet, maybe?"

"Could be," Dex murmured.

Dakota hid a grin. With the help of Bob, the hedgehog shifter, she and Dex had placed bets on their fight, figuring they had nothing to lose. She had put up all her savings, while Dex had bet the million he had stashed away, and they'd both doubled their money. Luckily, the bookies at the Scarlet Palace had paid up, even if Schiller had refused to award the additional million dollars in prize money.

No surprise, Dex had muttered on their way out of Vegas.

Still, they had plenty, Dakota figured. Dex alone had a cool two million — half of which he'd decided to keep, with the other half donated to the *Save the Florida Panther* foundation. Of course, Alon must have bet much more to come out with his windfall — enough to bankrupt Schiller and buy in to Scarlet Enterprises.

"It gets better." Karen chuckled. "*In a separate press release, Alon Edgar stated: 'The Scarlet Palace has always been a beacon of innovation and customer service. My team and I are simply carrying on those traditions in an exciting new direction. While continuing to offer the same great entertainment experiences as ever, we will introduce fully vegan, organic menus, plus 100% solar power and sustainable business practices. Our customers care about the planet, and we do too. Ladies and gentlemen, the future of Vegas is now!'*"

Karen ended with a flourish, and everyone laughed.

"You think it will be a success?" Trey asked.

Dakota shrugged. "It could."

"What really counts is running Schiller and his bloodsucking vampires out of business," Kaya said.

Dex nodded. "Last I heard from Bob, they're planning to turn the fighting pits into a luxury spa."

Everyone laughed, and Kaya went on. "So, no more fighting pits, no more blood orgies, no feasts." She put the word in air quotes. "None of us managed that — not me, not Trey, not Karen, or Tanner." Then she pointed at Dex and Dakota. "The world might not know it, but they have you to thank for that."

Dakota stuck up her hands. "They have Alon to thank. And you — all of you — for getting us out of there alive."

Karen grinned. "I think we can all take a little credit. Ready for a toast?"

She raised her beer bottle, and everyone followed suit.

"To soy-loving vampires. To Flying Aces Ranch. To a peaceful, happy existence far from Las Vegas."

Kaya raised her glass, taking it over from there. "To the next generation of Proulxs running the ranch. And who knows?" She winked at Trey. "Maybe another generation will come along soon."

Dakota smiled. Judging by the shine in Kaya's eyes, babies weren't too far off in Kaya and Trey's future. Karen and Tanner exchanged secret glances too, while Dex...

He slipped an arm over Dakota's shoulders and kissed her ear. "Someday, yes. But first..."

Her mind filled with steamy images straight from his.

"First, a lot of practice, huh?" she whispered.

He grinned. "That, and fixing up our cabin. Getting settled into our new jobs. Looking for our own property around here. Plus, you have to train Thunder, and—"

She cut him off there. "I get it, I get it. Plenty to handle for now. But someday..."

Dex sighed and nestled closer. "One someday at a time, okay? I'm still enjoying this one, my mate."

Sneak Peek: Lure of the Dragon

Nothing is forbidden to this elite corps of bodyguards and private eyes — except falling in love.

Good dragons? Bad dragons? Twenty-four hours ago, private chef Tessa Byrne didn't know about the terrifying world of shifters. Now she knows too much, like the fact that a ruthless dragon lord is determined to claim her — forever. Tessa flees to Maui, where sunny skies, swaying palms, and a handsome stranger conspire to play tricks with her heart. Can she truly trust Kai Llewellyn and his band of battle-hardened shapeshifters to save her from a gruesome fate?

Don't trust a human, and never, ever fall in love with one. Those are lessons Kai learned the hard way. But Tessa is different. Her emerald eyes mirror the mysterious pendant she wears, and her flaming red hair makes his heart race. Is his inner dragon just greedy for a new kind of treasure, or is Tessa his destined mate?

Books by Anna Lowe

Shifters in Vegas

Paranormal romance with a zany twist

Gambling on Trouble

Gambling on Her Dragon

Gambling on Her Bear

Gambling on Her Panther

Aloha Shifters - Jewels of the Heart

Lure of the Dragon (Book 1)

Lure of the Wolf (Book 2)

Lure of the Bear (Book 3)

Lure of the Tiger (Book 4)

Love of the Dragon (Book 5)

Lure of the Fox (Book 6)

Aloha Shifters - Pearls of Desire

Rebel Dragon (Book 1)

Rebel Bear (Book 2)

Rebel Lion (Book 3)

Rebel Wolf (Book 4)

Rebel Heart (A prequel to Book 5)

Rebel Alpha (Book 5)

Fire Maidens - Billionaires & Bodyguards

Fire Maidens: Paris (Book 1)

Fire Maidens: London (Book 2)

Fire Maidens: Rome (Book 3)

Fire Maidens: Portugal (Book 4)

Fire Maidens: Ireland (Book 5)

Fire Maidens: Scotland (Book 6)

Fire Maidens: Venice (Book 7)

Fire Maidens: Greece (Book 8)

Fire Maidens: Switzerland (Book 9)

The Wolves of Twin Moon Ranch

Desert Hunt (the Prequel)

Desert Moon (Book 1)

Desert Blood (Book 2)

Desert Fate (Book 3)

Desert Heart (Book 4)

Desert Rose (Book 5)

Desert Roots (Book 6)

Desert Yule (a short story)

Desert Wolf: Complete Collection (Four short stories)

Sasquatch Surprise (a Twin Moon spin-off story)

Blue Moon Saloon

Perfection (a short story prequel)

Damnation (Book 1)

Temptation (Book 2)

Redemption (Book 3)

Salvation (Book 4)

Deception (Book 5)

Celebration (a holiday treat)

Serendipity Adventure Romance

Off the Charts

Uncharted

Entangled

Windswept

Adrift

Travel Romance

Veiled Fantasies

Island Fantasies

www.annalowebooks.com

About the Author

USA Today and Amazon bestselling author Anna Lowe loves putting the "hero" back into heroine and letting location ignite a passionate romance. She likes a heroine who is independent, intelligent, and imperfect – a woman who is doing just fine on her own. But give the heroine a good man – not to mention a chance to overcome her own inhibitions – and she'll never turn down the chance for adventure, nor shy away from danger.

Anna loves dogs, sports, and travel – and letting those inspire her fiction. On any given weekend, you might find her hiking in the mountains or hunched over her laptop, working on her latest story. Either way, the day will end with a chunk of dark chocolate and a good read.

Visit AnnaLoweBooks.com

Printed in Great Britain
by Amazon